# Krampus &
# The Thief of
# Christmas

by Eldritch Black

# Krampus &
# The Thief of Christmas

Interior design by Eldritch Black
www.eldritchblack.com

Give feedback on the book at:
eldritch@eldritchblack.com

Twitter: @EldritchBlack

First Edition

Printed in the U.S.A

For Krampus, Father Christmas, & my secret helpers

# PROLOGUE

The man in the long red robe stood by the window as storm clouds rose from the south and a shadow fell across the land. He watched as the gathering darkness swallowed the crescent moon and extinguished the twinkling star. "It will be tonight then," he said. Black silhouettes dashed across the distant snowy landscape, like letters inked upon paper. They vanished beneath the city gates, then reappeared as they wound through the empty streets.

His spirits dropped and the room grew cold, despite the roaring fire blazing in the hearth. He jumped as someone rapped upon the door.

Eldos Stark, his faithful elven servant entered, a flicker of disgust upon his usually stony face. "You have visitors, m'lord."

"Show them in."

"Are you certain?" Stark raised a coppery eyebrow. "They're trolls."

"Trolls or not, please show them in." *For nothing will stop them from entering, if that is their will.*

Three grizzly wizened figures pushed past Stark, their dark garb leeching the color from the elf's bright green and red livery. Stark turned on his heels and retired to his quarters.

"Good eventide old Father Christmas," one of the trolls said, his black eyes narrowing below his wild, bushy eyebrows. He ran a grimy finger through his long beard and a slow, unpleasant sneer creased his face. "The master awaits you upon the hill near the border."

"Very well. I'll make my way there."

The trolls continued to stare in silence.

"Fine," Father Christmas said. "I'll travel with you, if that is your will."

The trolls gave a sharp nod and turned. Their long pointed shoes clacked and thumped down the stone steps as he followed.

A mighty black sled harnessed with a team of six wolves waited just outside the palace door. Their fur was the color of charcoal and sleet, their eyes flashes of green. Father Christmas climbed aboard and wedged himself on the seat beside two of the trolls. The third sat cross legged upon a pile of furs and seized the reins.

They travelled in silence through the city and out the gate, crossing the snowy wastes toward the great forest.

Father Christmas shivered as they passed beneath the trees. The lands had never looked so dark or so fearsome as they did upon this freezing, bitter night.

. . .

The wolves raced across the frozen lake and up the tall snowy hill that stood on the border between the land of Christmas and the black lands beyond. A giant pine tree rose from the crest and he saw Krampus leaning back against its trunk. He wore a long sleek black coat and his bright yellow-orange eyes gleamed below the dark silhouette of his horns. Krampus gave Father Christmas a fox-like grin. "You missed our last meeting." His voice was low yet gruff. "And the one before that."

"I was preoccupied."

Krampus nodded. "I see you've been living the good life. You've certainly grown in width since we last met. But your tailor has done a wonderful job of tucking most of it away." Krampus stroked the tip of his long goatee beard. "So you built your machine then."

"Indeed. It's been bliss. My elves and I only have to put in a few nights worth of work now. When I think back on how we used to toil away for months on end…. Well, let's just say, we've come to appreciate the same extended break you yourself enjoy for the better part of the year."

Krampus's smile widened, revealing his long, curved teeth. "Does it still irk you that my role only requires a performance on one evening of the year? I'd work every single night if it were up to me. Because unlike you, I relish my responsibilities."

"If only we could have swapped places," Father Christmas said.

"Quite. I'd sell my ancestor's teeth for the reputation you enjoy. Hardly a soul knows who I am, and those who do are terrified. I'm as reviled as you are loved."

Father Christmas gave a short, bitter laugh. "I may well be known, but there's plenty who don't even believe I exist. I'm lampooned, made into a caricature, my identity assumed by countless imposters. Would you settle for that?"

"Perhaps," Krampus said. "But I didn't summon you here for this."

"So there's no time for idle conversation and friendship?"

Krampus's smile faded. "I want my gold. Every single gram. A year and a day has passed. You promised I'd have it back within six moons, when you borrowed it to build that machine. It's given you the easy life you dreamed of, as made evident by the girth of your belly, but now it's time for you to repay me."

"I...I can't. Not tonight. Give me more time and I'll have your gold. And more still. I'll-"

Krampus's tail lashed the tree trunk and a long claw caught the moonlight as he held up a single finger. "I've given you more than enough time. A deal is a deal."

"I'm sorry." Father Christmas felt his face flush. "I don't have the means to pay you. Not right now."

"Then when?" Krampus's purred but a hard edge crept into his voice.

Father Christmas shrugged. "Don't worry, everything will be well. I'll work night and day-"

"Time has run out." Krampus loomed over him. "If you can't pay me now, then we'll have to leave it for chance to decide." He pulled a deck of cards from his pocket. "We'll play a simple game. We will each cut the deck and whoever holds the highest card will win."

"Win what?" A sinking feeling passed through Father Christmas.

"If you win you can keep my gold without any further complaint or demand. But if I win, you hand me the key to Christmas."

"But it's not mine to give."

"And neither is my gold yours to keep," Krampus growled. "Now play the game, allow chance to decide. The deck is stacked in your favor, luck favors the good and noble, and I'm neither of those things."

"And if I refuse?"

"Then by the rock and the stone, I'll have my trolls throw you into the darkest pit beneath my mountain. And there you'll fester until I gather the goodwill to release you."

"I see," Father Christmas said. The hill and the dark lands surrounding it were making him feel very small indeed. Small and vulnerable. He averted his gaze as the trolls glared down at him, their eyes as hard as flint. "Let's play then." Father Christmas said.

Krampus nodded and held up his deck of cards while lightning lashed the clouds and thunder rumbled across the lands.

# CHAPTER ONE

No matter what her uncle said, Gabrielle Greene was certain she'd heard wolves. She gazed through the flurries of snow that fell like soft curled feathers, toward the distant wooded hills and mountains. An icy wind screeched from the east and with it came another chorus of howls.

She glanced to the jagged mountains, and imagined the beasts descending, lean and grey, with slathering tongues and wicked-cruel teeth. She wished she could howl back, to tell them to keep away from her and Percival. To warn them that even though she lacked claws and fangs, if they threatened her or her brother, she'd tear them apart.

But if they wished to devour her cousin Matilda, she was fine with that.

"Mind out little girl." A man in a long coat bustled past Gabrielle and hurried into a bright snug shop.

"I'm not a little girl," Gabrielle called out. "But you're definitely an idiot." She muttered as she swiped a snow flake from the tip of her nose. It seemed like it had been snowing from the moment they'd arrived, and even though they had only been in this town for a few weeks, it felt like years. "Is it ever going to stop?" she asked, half expecting her brother to chime in.

*I wish we were anywhere but here.* Gabrielle had lost count of the times she'd made that wish. She was completely sick of this strange, creepy place.

A din of rattling chains broke her thoughts. It was time to go home.

Gabrielle glanced at the bookshop, expecting to find Percival with his nose pressed against its window, but there was no sign of him. "Percival?" She checked the shops. He wasn't in any of them. "How many times have I told you about wandering off?" she whispered, as she scoured the snow for his footprints.

A cry rang out, and then it was gone. It came again, blown along with the wind as it whistled down a nearby street. Gabrielle glanced at the street sign with its odd, foreign words, and she knew exactly where Percival had gone.

She ran down the narrow lane, passing coffee shops, chocolatiers, bars and boutiques. Then she spotted Percival, standing near the toy shop window. Two older kids loomed over him and one tugged at his satchel.

"Get off!" Percival cried.

The boy let go of the strap, sending Percival flying against the window. He struck it with a dull thud. Their laughter grew shrill as Percival fell, and lay crumpled in the snow. Percival held his hand up as the boy leaped towards him. The boy drew back his fist but froze as he spotted Gabrielle thundering along the street towards him. "Leave him alone!" she growled.

The boys watched her from below their hoods, their expressions sullen. But when she stepped into the light of the shop window, they turned and fled.

"Are you okay, Perce?" Gabrielle helped him to his feet.

He nodded, his face either red from the struggle, or from embarrassment. Or both. He wiped his mousy-brown hair from his eyes. "I'm fine."

The boys stood at the end of the narrow street, watching. Then one of them leaned down and moments later a snow ball hurtled towards her. Gabrielle sidestepped. It landed upon the ground with a soft thump and broke apart like a lump of confetti. "Halfwit." Gabrielle's breath billowed from her mouth like dragon smoke as she whisked the snow from Percy's sleeve. She just wanted to get home and take her wet socks off. But the boys were now compacting snow into balls of ice in their padded gloves, and she knew they wouldn't stop. Not until she confronted them and provided proof of her monstrous reputation. "Go home, Percival. Don't dawdle."

"Ignore them."

"I can't." She stood her ground as another snowball whizzed past her head. Gabrielle waited for the next to fall at her feet, before running straight at them. They fled, their boots better suited to the icy ground than hers, their jackets buffering them against the screeching wind. Unlike Gabrielle's limp, ragged coat and her hand-me-down shoes. She pulled her scarf over her mouth and sprinted down the lane, the falling snow glistening around her like static on an old television screen.

The boys ducked around a corner at the end of the street. Gabrielle followed just in time to see them vanish down a gloomy alleyway. She slowed as she reached it, half expecting them to leap out and pelt her with ice-balls. Because that was what she would have done if the tables were turned.

The alley was empty.

Gabrielle ran past the dark doorways and frosted windows. Their mocking laughter seemed further away now. She emerged into a lane of closed shops, their interiors filled with formless shapes and restless shadows. It was an eerie place and her fury began to wane. She turned back and tramped through the snow, eager to be back among the warm glow of the street lights.

. . .

Percival was gone by the time Gabrielle reached the toy shop and his footprints, with the distinctive star-shaped tread in the heels, led toward the market place. There was still a small circle of condensation on the shop window where he had stood and Gabrielle could see the ornate ship-in-a-bottle he'd been obsessing over since they'd first arrived. Why it sparked his imagination, she had no idea, but it did. She'd lost count of how many times he'd mentioned its intricate sails, and the tiny wooden captain and sailors. And how he suspected they'd sail away if they were ever free of the bottle. And how they most likely came alive at midnight and plotted their escape to distant shores filled with treasure and glory.

Gabrielle checked the tag to see if the price had been reduced. It hadn't, but the fact the ship was still there meant she still had a chance to earn enough to buy it before Christmas.

She walked toward the high street, smiling as she imagined the look on Percival's face when he unwrapped it on Christmas morning. "Hey!" Gabrielle jumped back as a passing car splattered her with wet icy slush.

The market square was busy with tired-eyed locals and bright faced tourists, their cheeks rosy from either the cold winter weather or their own festive gluttony.

"Hey!"

Gabrielle turned to find a tall, fidgety looking boy approaching her. His hair appeared grey in the darkness below his hood. "Gabrielle Greene, right?" He used the same broken English as the other locals.

"I might be. Why?"

As he inclined his head, the shadows from his hood crept over his eyes. "I heard you can make problems go away. Is that right?" He stopped talking as a stream of people and a blast of jazz music spilled out from a nearby coffee shop.

"Not here," Gabrielle said. "Meet me at the library tomorrow. Eleven o'clock. Bring money."

"Right." The boy loped away.

A rush of excitement prickled through Gabrielle. Word was still spreading, just as she'd hoped it would. She could still remember the first kid who had approached her when she'd first arrived in the city. A pudgy faced girl who had asked Gabrielle where she was from. And how her eyes had gleamed when Gabrielle had told her. At first Gabrielle had been flattered by the girl's interest. Until it became clear that the only thing she required from Gabrielle was for her to take the blame for a spree of thefts from the chocolatiers. In return Gabrielle received a payment. A very generous payment.

There had been no reason she could think of not to take it. It wasn't as if she'd be staying in town for very long, and she could always do with money. But that had only been the start of her strange new venture and soon it seemed as if all the kids in the city needed someone to take the blame for their wrongdoings.

Gabrielle crossed the road. She was startled as a high pitched scream came from the market square. Within moments the scream became laughter.

A crowd of tourists surged through the market. Many clutched decorated cups, some in the shape of long red socks or scarlet and green striped canes. The scents of cinnamon, candied fruits, mulled wine and fried sausages laced the air. Gleaming festive baubles and tinsel hung from the stalls and glistened in the evening light. There were all manner of handmade goods on sale; blown glass stars, carved wooden nutcrackers, waxy scented candles and glittery holiday cards. Garlands and Christmas lights were strung up everywhere, twinkling silver, white, gold and red. Streams of voices rose around Gabrielle, tourists, shoppers, and vendors cajoling and barking for attention.

She hurried on, eager to get to the other side of the market, but as she passed by a carousel of painted horses, she froze as something sprang from the gloom.

The creature towered over her, horns jutting from its long, furry head. Fiery red eyes stared down from above its long wolfish snout. The beast brandished a clutch of birch sticks as its tail sloshed through the snow.

It roared and bore down upon her, cackling as its claws reached for her face.

# CHAPTER TWO

Gabrielle wheeled around as another beast leaped out and bore down on her. This one had tar-black eyes, curved white fangs and a split tongue that hung to its matted fur chest. It roared and laughed, its voice distinctly human. Gabrielle jumped as someone behind her screamed. A group of tourists cowered in mock terror as a ruddy-faced man took photographs of one of the creatures. It flaunted the chains around its neck as it posed for the camera.

"This place is insane." Gabrielle muttered as even more monsters jumped out from behind the stalls. Some wore plain furry getups with horns, but others had clearly invested a lot of money in their costumes. One had flashing red eyes, and frightening make-up that must have taken hours to apply.

Gabrielle wondered what they were supposed to be, and what any of this had to do with Christmas. She was furious with herself for being startled by such ridiculous costumes, and as another creature thundered towards her, she folded her arms and refused to move. It grinned and shook a bundle of twigs at her as it bounded away, provoking another chorus of screams. Gabrielle hurried through the market. She crossed the road and finally, the hubbub receded behind her.

The streetlights on her uncle's road were dim and barely cut through the gloom to the blue-grey snow mounded along the sidewalk below. Gabrielle checked to see if her uncle's car was parked in its usual space. It wasn't.

"Great."

But the light in Percival's room was on and she hoped he'd gotten home before the monsters had invaded the market place. He was easily scared and his nerves were far more fragile than hers.

Uncle Florian's house looked as decrepit as ever, like a rotten tooth amongst the tall pristine white buildings surrounding it. Strings of golden lights twinkled around the neighbors' windows, but Uncle Florian's were dark and empty and the plants in his snow-drowned garden bowed under the weight of the white blanket that covered them. Not a single wisp of smoke issued from his crooked chimney, which meant the fireplace still hadn't been fixed and they were in for another chilly night.

Gabrielle sighed as she followed Percival's footprints to the front door and let herself into the house. She stomped her feet until all the snow fell away and glistened upon the woven mat. Her fingers ached with cold as she pulled her shoes off, and her damp socks hung limp from her toes. Light flickered from the living room and voices jabbered from the television, their language clipped and foreign. Gabrielle opened the door and tip-toed through the room.

She almost made it to the door on the other side.

"There you are." Matilda turned from the sofa. Her piggy eyes widened above her button nose, and her thin lips drew back to reveal the dull metal braces encasing her teeth. She held out a bony hand.

"What?" Gabrielle asked.

"You know what. Three people called to complain today. One about a smashed window, one about graffiti, and the one about a boy buried up to his neck in snow. His mother said someone painted his face bright green like a Christmas bauble. I took their names and phone numbers, do you want them? Or should I give them to my father?" She splayed her bony fingers wider.

Gabrielle pulled a handful of money from her pocket and smacked it down into her cousin's palm. Matilda counted the notes, before slipping them into her purse.

They both turned to the television as someone roared.

A reporter stood in a market. She held a microphone out before someone dressed up like one of the monsters from the Christmas market. They grimaced, revealing a forked tongue and fangs.

"Oh look, soon it will be Krampusnight. As I'm sure you'll find out," Matilda said. "He'll definitely come calling for you, so you better lock your door. And your windows. Or maybe he'll slither down the chimney." Her eyes gleamed as she gazed at the hole in the living room wall. The fireplace had been removed for repairs, leaving an ominous dark space below the cracked tiles.

Gabrielle didn't want to give her cousin the satisfaction of asking what Krampusnight was. So she shrugged and left the room, but not before Matilda added, "You'll see. If Krampus is coming for anyone, it's going to be you!"

. . .

The hallway was as cold and drafty as ever. A slight trace of heat rose from the radiators, but not enough to make a difference. Gabrielle hoped her uncle would be home soon, that way she could sit in the living room where it was marginally warmer. Plus Matilda would have to be polite to them, because she always wore her fake model daughter mask in front of her father. "Stupid, idiot, fraud." Gabrielle pushed her bedroom door open.

It was just as drafty and cold as the hallway and the large open space made her sparse belongings look even more pitiful than they were. The furniture was old, rickety and covered in dust, no matter how often Gabrielle cleaned it. And it was probably dated from the last century. Nothing about the room could have been more different from her room back home.

She wished she was there now, lying on her own bed in the warmth, with no stupid vindictive cousin to worry about. But thanks to her parents' constant arguments and their endless quest to resolve their differences, she was stuck here. Why were they so selfish? Why was everyone so selfish? Everyone except Percival, at least most of the time, and of course her Uncle Florian.

Gabrielle pulled the curtains across the bay window that overlooked the back garden and the alley and houses beyond. She put on another sweater and rubbed her hands together. She was about to pull the duvet over herself when she heard what sounded very much like a sob coming from her brother's room. As Gabrielle stole over to the door to listen, her foot struck the creaky floorboard and the sobbing stopped.

She rapped her knuckles on the flaking paint. "Perce?"

There was no answer.

Gabrielle opened the door.

Percival was sitting at his desk, his coloring book wide open. As he turned to face her, a pen rolled from the desk and fell upon the lumpy carpet. He smiled, but his lips quivered.

"Are you okay?"

"Yes." Percival nodded. "Why?"

"Was it the boys who tried to steal your bag? They got away, but the next time I see them I'll blacken their eyes and they'll both look like pandas. Or zombies. Or zombie pandas."

"I don't care about them. I'm used to it. No one in this place likes us."

"That's not true, Uncle Florian likes us."

"But he's never here."

"He has to work, Perce. Although I don't know why, seeing as he says no one ever goes into his shop. But he said he's taking Christmas off, and that's only three weeks away. And then we can go out and do stuff and Matilda will have to stop hassling us."

"I want to go home, I miss mum and dad." The corners of Percival lips turned down.

Gabrielle sighed. "They'll be back soon and then we can go home."

"They won't be back for," Percival checked the huge advent calendar their uncle had made for him, "ages."

"The time will pass quickly, I promise. And then we'll be back at school and you'll be wishing it was Christmas again. We should try to enjoy being here, we've never been anywhere like this before."

"And I never want to be anywhere like it again."

"Why don't you open another door on your calendar? It's almost tomorrow. Give or take five or six hours."

"I..." Percival's face reddened. He stooped to pick his pens up from the floor. "I've opened them all already."

"You've opened all the doors, all the way to Christmas Eve?"

Percival nodded.

"But today's only the fourth." Gabrielle was about to chastise him, when his face fell even further. "Well I haven't opened mine yet. Do you want to do it for me?"

Percival gave her a crooked smile. The same one that always melted her heart, no matter how irritating he was being. She opened her door, switched the lamp on and shined the light upon her wall. The advent calendar was painted to depict a snowy wonderland with an ice cream mountain top, and a forest of chocolate brown pine trees. A huge moon, pitted with craters, shone in the twinkling night sky and illuminated the whole scene.

Gabrielle watched as Percival patiently traced his finger along the glitter that highlighted the snow drifts and a tiny dusting of sparkles fell down to the floor. He searched the calendar for the door that marked the fourth of December. Their uncle's stunning craftsmanship and eye for detail had ensured that each little opening was artfully hidden. Percival's eyes gleamed as he pulled and prized at the seam in the trunk of a pine tree. Light spilled from the calendar, a tiny clockwork whirled and the chime of bells rang. Even now, the lights and sounds made Gabrielle smile. She'd never seen any other calendar like it.

Percival opened the door and removed a candy owl covered in golden foil. He unwrapped the chocolate, snapped it in two and offered half to Gabrielle.

"No, you can have it."

Percival didn't need telling twice. Within seconds the owl was gone and the only evidence of its existence was a smudge of chocolate around his lips.

"Now, go finish coloring your picture and stop worrying,

all right? Uncle Florian will be home soon and hopefully he'll get the heating working before we all freeze to death."

The moment Percival shut his door, Gabrielle fell onto her lumpy bed and closed her eyes. She was exhausted, and still unnerved. The masquerading beasts in the market place had unsettled her. As had Percival's growing anxiety.

And then there was Matilda's ominous warning...

*Oh yes, if Krampus is coming for anyone, it's going to be you!*

# CHAPTER THREE

Dinner that night was a large pizza in an oily box hand delivered by their uncle. Gabrielle had to stop herself from retching as Matilda beamed and set the table with a sickeningly sweet smile. For now, her true evil was hidden behind her mask, but it wouldn't last long.

Uncle Florian swept his floppy grey hair back from his thick black glasses and ran a squeaky wheel across the pizza. He broke it into cheesy mushroom and ham triangles, and handed Gabrielle a plate. "And how was your day?" he asked.

"Good, thanks." Gabrielle decided not to mention the kids who had bullied Percival, or the people in the market square dressed as beasts. Uncle Florian looked exhausted, the bags below his eyes more pronounced than ever. He smiled, as always trying to make the best of things, and this only made Gabrielle more determined to try and do the same.

"Your mother called the shop," Uncle Florian said. "She's going to phone you tonight, if she can. She said things are going well with your father. I think everything will be resolved soon and you should both be home by January."

"Oh, that's a shame." Matilda gave Gabrielle a sharp kick in the ankle, her sneer glistening with grease. "But at least they'll be here for Krampus night."

"What's Krampus night?" Percival asked.

"It's the night when all the bad kids are taken away and punished, and–"

"That's enough, thank you Matilda." Uncle Florian set his knife and fork down. He gave Percival a gentle smile. "It's just an old legend. Nothing for you to worry about. Besides, you're good kids."

Matilda flashed Gabrielle a knowing look. "Yes, father, you're probably right. I'm sure the great beast Krampus won't need to come here. Right?"

"Enough, please," Uncle Florian gave Matilda a pointed look and the remainder of the meal passed in silence.

"Help me clear the table, Perce." Gabrielle said as they finished. She picked up the plates, while Percival carried the empty pizza box into the kitchen. Gabrielle washed the dishes and Percival dried. By the time they returned to the living room, her uncle was fast asleep in his chair, his mouth open, his glasses hanging from his nose. Matilda sat in front of the television, brushing her hair and gazing blankly at the screen.

"Come on Percival," Gabrielle whispered, "let's leave them to it."

*Before that rotten cow tries to put any more nightmares into our heads.*

· · ·

Gabrielle woke to a clattering din in the middle of the night. Her heart beat hard as she sat up in the dark. Fragments of her dream swirled through her mind; a dream of beastly figures hiding behind shifting trees. Her eyes darted from the wardrobe to the window as the noise erupted again. It sounded like a dustbin lid falling. Gabrielle glanced between the curtains. The bare tree branches were perfectly still. There was no wind. She climbed from the bed's snug warmth and pulled the curtain aside.

Her breath snagged in her chest.

A tall lean woman stooped in the middle of the garden. She wore a scarlet woolen coat and her face was as white as the snow surrounding her black boots. A jumble of long blue-black hair spilled from the brim of her fur hat, almost obscuring her dark, narrowed eyes. She raised her head and sniffed and her gaze shot to the window.

Gabrielle gasped and ducked back into the shadows.

The woman reached out with a gloved hand and splayed her fingers against the window. The thin film of ice that coated the glass crackled and jagged crystals spread across it as she leaned closer in. Her nostrils flared and she sniffed again; Gabrielle could hear her panting breath. It was as loud and frantic as a hound's. The woman pressed her hand hard against the glass and the ice grew thicker and thicker.

It was all Gabrielle could do to contain her scream as the woman growled and peered through the frost. Her black eyes slowly roved across the room. She muttered as she turned and waded through the snow, making her way toward the back of an old fashioned ice cream van parked in the alley between houses. Images of cones, gum balls and wafers adorned its side, encircling an impish face with gobstoppers for eyes and a trickle of jam for a mouth. At least, Gabrielle hoped it was jam. "Ice creams?" she whispered. "At midnight? In winter?

Why would-"

Then four tiny figures scrambled out of a nearby house. They wore long black duffel coats with hoods that obscured their faces and they carried a large plump burlap sack between them. Something moved and writhed inside and Gabrielle was sure she could hear a muffled cry. The figures tossed the sack into the back of the van and climbed in behind it.

The woman closed and bolted the van doors before climbing into the driver's seat. Moments later the van spluttered to life and trundled away, its snow chains clinking and churning the slush and mud as it rolled down the alley and vanished from view.

Gabrielle's mind whirled. She thought about waking Uncle Florian and telling him what she'd seen.

But what had she seen? A prank, or a kidnapping? Or was it just her imagination, as wild as ever? She looked toward the houses across the alley, but they remained still and dark, their black eye-like windows gazing emptily back at her.

She tugged the curtain closed and climbed into the warmth of her bed, her mind racing until she finally fell into a deep, troubled sleep.

# CHAPTER FOUR

Krampus grinned at his reflection in the full length gold-leafed looking glass. How fine his teeth were in their various shades of white, yellow and black, their tips perfectly sharp. How resplendent his eyes, the color of fiery suns flecked with topaz, their black slits as vibrant as ever.

He stuck out his scarlet forked tongue and plucked a flea from the wild fur upon his chest. His tongue crushed the flea, before popping it into his mouth. It then snaked up and licked away a dusting of ash from the immense black horns that crowned his head. Then he turned to gaze at his tail; time hadn't stolen even a millimeter from its majesty.

"I'm in my prime," he growled, his voice as smooth as a silken noose. "The king of winter!" His cloven hooves clattered on the polished obsidian floor as he approached his throne. It was made of the darkest ebony and ever-bright embers burnt on the ends of its tall twisted spikes. He sat and gazed into the roaring fireplace. The flames danced like molten waves as the blazing heat filled the vast throne room. He turned toward a pair of double doors, crested with the letter K formed from thorns and barbs, and smiled as he clapped his hands. "Let the gifting begin!"

Bells rang, their chimes deep and resonant. Then the doors flew open and a procession of trolls entered, dragging wriggling sacks behind them.

Krampus's smile widened. He loved his trolls. They were like miniature versions of himself with their wild black hair and fangs. But he loved them even more when they brought presents. "What rare and wonderful gifts have you got for me this year, Curdle?" Krampus asked the first troll.

"Wicked little sprites, sire. So wicked, that were you to chop them in two, you'd find veins of wickedness running through them like minerals through rock," Curdle replied in his low, rasping voice. "And there's plenty more coming. It's going to take several train loads to get them all here."

The sacks thrashed and squirmed as Curdle and the other trolls cut the strings that tied them shut. A pair of slippers emerged from the first, followed by a boy dressed in red and blue pajamas. The child's eyes grew wild as they fell upon Krampus, then he let out a shriek that echoed off the cavern walls.

"Place them in a line," Krampus ordered.

The trolls stooped down, grasping at slippered feet as they pulled the other children from their sacks. Howls and whimpers filled the cavern as the trolls shoved them into a cowering line.

Krampus nodded contentedly. "Their squeals and screeches are music to my ears. A cacophony of wondrous sounds. Thank you, children. Thank you one and all." He stood before a boy with rapidly blinking eyes and a matted mass of straw-blonde hair. Krampus leaned down and sniffed the child's ear. "Such a succulent bouquet of wickedness."

He continued along the line. Some of the children wept and others tried to run but the trolls hooked shepherd's crooks around their throats and held them straight.

"Yes," Krampus continued, "a fine year for roguery, a veritable vintage indeed. I detect a hint of moldy cheese aged in the summer sun. And there - a hint of stale socks left under a bed for no less than a year. Ah, and the scent of this one is not unlike goat breath at dawn. Good, good!" Krampus rattled the rusted chains he wore across his shoulders and turned back to the trolls. "Now, take these miscreants away and ensure each receives a fitting punishment. I'd mete them out myself, but I have more pressing concerns. Curdle, wait here."

One by one the trolls led the whimpering children from the chamber. Krampus waited for the enormous doors to clang shut, before turning to Curdle. "That was a very good yield. But tell me...where's the wickedest child of all? That really bad one. I didn't detect the beat of her blackened heart amongst those odious souls." Krampus ran his forked tongue across his fangs. An old sign of irritation.

"No, sire." Curdle rubbed his hands briskly. His pointed shoes were aimed towards the doors, as if he intended to fly from the room. "I'm afraid we don't have her yet."

"It's Krampusnight. Why isn't she here?"

"We...we tried to get her, but we couldn't pick up her scent. Not I, nor Madam Grystle caught wind of her. Not even Helibish, and he can smell a dead rat through five miles of sewerage."

"Didn't my informants provide a location?" Krampus's voice was a malicious purr.

"Of course, sire. We know exactly where she lives. Her and her pestilent little brother."

"Then bring her here at once! We've all been out tonight, gathering bushels full of these rotten little apples. All you had to do was grab a single girl."

"But we can't get her, sire. There's not even the slightest whiff of wickedness about her and without that we can't breach the house or pull her from her snug little bed."

"She must be using sorcery. A powerful magic we cannot detect. At least not yet." Krampus tugged the end of his beard. "You mentioned a brother."

"Yes. His soul is feather light, and as sickly sweet as honey." The troll's face soured. "A most revolting child."

"Is he close to his sister?"

"As close as a fly to fresh muck."

"Since we don't have the measure of this girl's sorcerous defenses, maybe we can use the little brother as bait. Bring him, and the girl will follow."

"But how?" the troll asked. "There's not even a scrap of wickedness in him."

"Then change that. Make him err. That isn't beyond your capabilities. Is it?"

"I'll try," Curdle agreed. "And we can-"

"Do not try!" Krampus roared. "Trying is as weak as wet paper. Just. Bring. The. Boy. To. Me."

"I'll do my very best. I swear it."

Krampus rolled his eyes. "Try? Do my best? Lily-livered words. Go to Madam Grystle, tell her what I need. She'll snag and snaffle the boy. Then his sister will follow and I will have what's mine. This is going to be my year, Curdle. The year I get my revenge on the fat one once and for all! You'll see, the colors of Christmas will turn from red and green to deepest black. Yes, this will be the year of Krampus, and all those who serve him!"

"A most stirring speech, master."

"Enough lickspittle. Enough prattle and toadying. Fetch the brother, that's how I'll catch my thief of Christmas!"

# CHAPTER FIVE

When Gabrielle had woken that morning, it had taken a few moments for her to recall the cloudy events of the night before. The woman at the window and the strange childlike figures that had pulled a wriggling sack from the neighbor's house. She'd dressed quickly and rushed to tell her uncle about it, but he'd already left for work.

Breakfast had been a miserable affair, with Matilda taking every opportunity to mention Krampusnight. All the while fixing Gabrielle with a smug, horrible grin. Naturally her comments had led to Percival asking what Krampusnight was, and Gabrielle rushed to get him out of the room before Matilda could reply.

Now as Gabrielle sat in the library, away from the cold drear of the house and her cousin's endless malice, she allowed herself to relax. The library was warm and well lit, people only spoke in hushed voices and the staff were kind and courteous. Percival was safely tucked away in the children's section leafing through the comics.

Gabrielle glanced through a book while she waited. Moments later the library doors opened and the hooded boy from the previous night bustled in. He gazed from the bookshelves to the people reading on the sofas as if he'd never seen anything so strange. Then his shifty eyes alighted on Gabrielle. She nodded for him to follow her and she made her way to the end of an empty aisle. Gabrielle pulled out a section of books, checking the adjoining aisle to make sure it was free of spies and interlopers.

The boy shifted his weight from one foot to the other.

"Have you brought the money?" Gabrielle asked. He dug into his pocket and pulled out a handful of notes. Gabrielle counted them. "I suppose that will do. Right, tell me what you've done."

The boy whispered his story in broken English.

"I see," Gabrielle said, as he finished. "Just out of interest, why did you set off fireworks in an old peoples' home?"

"I thought it would be funny."

"Was it?"

He shook his head. "Not really."

Gabrielle pursed her lips. She wasn't here to judge, she was here to provide a service. "Did anyone see you?"

"I don't know. Maybe the cameras?"

"Hmm. If someone owns up to it now, they probably won't bother checking them."

"Exactly." His eyes brightened.

"I'll go this afternoon."

"Thank you."

"I'm not doing it for charity. Listen, if you have any friends who need someone to take the blame, send them my way. Just as long as they've got money."

The boy nodded briskly. "You're very brave," he said.

"No I'm not. I don't live here so I'm not worried about getting a bad reputation. You misbehave, I take the blame, and we're all happy."

"But you are brave," the boy persisted. "Krampus…"

"I don't want to hear about that rubbish," Gabrielle said. But she still shivered as she thought back to those monsters in the market square.

*Oh yes, if Krampus is coming for anyone, it's going to be you!* "There's no such thing as Krampus," Gabrielle said.

"Isn't there?" The boy looked as if he were about to add something further, but a severe-looking librarian appeared. The light flashed across her glasses as she approached, giving each of them a disapproving glance.

The boy nodded to Gabrielle and shot down the aisle, giving the librarian as wide a berth as possible.

. . .

It only just began to dawn on Madam Grystle, now that she'd been following the insufferable child for hours, that this was an utterly fruitless task. Mostly the little prig clung to his sister like mud to a heel, but even when they did separate she just couldn't seem to get a hold of him.

Like now as he stood before a shop window, gazing through the glass like a goldfish. Madam Grystle tried to grasp the scruff of his neck, but she snatched her hand away. The reek of his goodness almost made her double over and retch. It hung about him like a sainted shroud while the air around him glittered and gleamed in the most disorienting way. She was glad for the dark glasses she'd stolen, but even they couldn't stop the boy's aura from causing her eyes to ache. This really was the most wretched task.

Madam Grystle leaned over as another wave of nausea passed through her. She tucked a stray strand of blue-black hair back below her fur cap. The boy was so close, so alone...

She glanced across the street. The trolls, Uffle and Gawp, bounced on their heels as they stood watching. They looked like a pair of hairy children, their duffle coats pulled up to their throats, their wild black hair barely contained beneath their hoods. Uffle, the more impatient of the pair, held up his gloved hands in exasperation.

What did he expect her to do? Seize the child? As if that hadn't been her first instinct. But she couldn't. If she tried, she'd singe her fingers just as badly as if she'd plunged them into a pot of molten sugar. Her hands still bore the scars from the last time she tried to nab a sweet little innocent, and even though it was centuries ago now, they still twinged during the summer's rancid heat.

Madam Grystle stepped back and took a deep breath. The sky was lowering. It would soon be night. It was time. She walked past the boy and dropped a handful of coins upon the ground. Take them. Madam Grystle crossed her fingers so hard they ached. *Take the money, child. Take what is not yours.*

"Excuse me, Miss!"

Madam Grystle froze as a stinky little hand tugged her sleeve. She whirled round to find the boy standing before her, a sickeningly sweet smile upon his face and the coins gleaming upon his palm. "You dropped your money, Miss."

"No," Madam Grystle tried a smile. "I'm sure I didn't."

"But you did," the boy said. "I saw it happen."

Madam Grystle tried to pull her gloved hand away, but the wretched child had already dropped the coins into her palm. She growled, revealing her tusks. "That could have been your money, boy. But nothing's going to darken that festering light that encircles your head like flies around-"

"Perce?"

A chime of bells rang out as the girl came out of the shop and approached them. She was young, but her eyes were old and clever. As wise as a crow and as suspicious as a feral cat. Madam Grystle hid her tusks as best she could before offering the girl a smile.

She crossed the street and joined Uffle and Gawp. "I tried," Madam Grystle growled, "but the boy's not going to be turned. At least not by a handful of coins,"

"The master-" Gawp began.

"Your master," Madam Grystle reminded him. "Not mine. Krampus and I are partners and both of us have an equal stake and claw in the fat hide of Christmas."

"But we can't take the girl, and we can't take the boy," Uffle rolled his eyes. "So what are we to do? Return empty handed and get thrashed with birch sticks? Or be put on nose scraping duties for the rest of the month?"

"We'll not return empty handed," Madam Grystle promised. "No, we'll get that little brat by hook or crook. Even if it has to wait till tomorrow. And when we do, his sister will follow. And then we'll soon be rid of the tyranny of Christmas."

. . .

Gabrielle took Percival home. She waited until he was happily playing in his bedroom, before slipping out to make good on her promises.

First she stopped at the cake shop and made a full apology for the theft of a tray of apple strudels. It was touch and go, the florid-faced baker nearly called the police, but eventually she let Gabrielle go with a stark warning.

Next, was the museum where Gabrielle apologized for the addition of a pair of fake rabbit ears to the statue of the city's founding father. That and the sign hung around his neck that translated to 'Founding idiot, and turnip maker'. The museum curator's outrage along with his stutter caused the rebuke to take the better part of an hour to be delivered. Gabrielle gave him her uncle's phone number and explained that all complaints must be directed to her aunt Matilda.

Finally, she'd made her way to the old people's home for the apology she'd been dreading the most. As much as she liked a good prank, it was painfully obvious that letting off fireworks amongst frail people with weak and faulty hearts was not the best idea. Which was exactly what the stern faced Care Officer had told Gabrielle. "I should call the police," she'd told Gabrielle in a harsh, clipped voice. "Give me one reason not to. Go on!"

Which was why Gabrielle had come to spend the rest of the afternoon cleaning every inch of their huge kitchen until each of the knives, forks and spoons gleamed and all the work tops were spotless. Finally the Care Officer dismissed her, and Gabrielle left the home's cloying warmth for the dark icy walk back to Uncle Florian's.

. . .

Gabrielle slept soundly until she was woken by a rapping upon her window. According to the clock it was nearly midnight, so she pulled the covers over her head, and willed the world to leave her alone, if only for a few hours.

She fell back to sleep, but was jolted awake again by a sound of rustling.

It was coming from her room.

The squeaky floorboard near Percival's room creaked. Was he up? Gabrielle pulled the covers from her face to see a figure flitting past her bed.

It was too tall to be Percival.

# CHAPTER SIX

It was still dark when Gabrielle got up, but a few fingers of dawn stretched over the horizon. As she reached for her dressing gown, her eyes fell on her advent calendar. Every single door was open and empty.

Gabrielle shoved the adjoining door to Percival's room and stormed in. His face was stained with blue marker as he glanced up from his coloring book.

"I said you could open one door on my calendar. One, not all of them." Gabrielle did her best to keep her tone even.

Percival's face turned red beneath the inky blue streaks. "I didn't touch your calendar."

Gabrielle marched over to his desk. A small mountain of gold foil wrappers gleamed in the waste basket. "Where did these come from then?" She pulled out a handful and let them fall upon the floor.

"I don't know. They're not mine."

"Don't lie, Percival."

"I. Didn't. Eat. Your. Chocolates!"

"Of course you didn't. It was probably the tooth fairy. She must have accidentally collected a sweet tooth. I'm getting sick of this, Percival. As if I don't already do everything for you, now you're lying to me?"

"I'm not lying. And I don't ask you to do anything. You're always poking your nose into everything, you never trust me with nothing."

"I think you meant, I don't trust you with *anything.*"

"You think you're so clever, don't you!" Percival swiped his hands across the desk, sending his pens and markers flying.

"I wouldn't have to spend all my time worrying about you if you didn't act like a helpless little child, would I?" Gabrielle stormed from his room and slammed the door behind her. She climbed into her bed and pulled the covers over her head, blotting out the world and its stupidity and turmoil.

. . .

Percival still blazed with fury as he climbed out of his bedroom window and dropped into the snow. He slid the window closed and made his way across the garden to the pavement.

It was early. Too early. A few people milled around the market and delivery drivers double parked outside the shops, their trucks wheezing and hissing like ancient beasts. Percival hurried past, his feet taking him in no particular direction. He glanced back to see if Gabrielle was following. She wasn't. She probably didn't even know he'd gone yet. He allowed himself an angry smile as he imagined her panic once she realized he was gone. "She deserves it," Percival muttered through his scarf.

His anger abated a little as he slowed to avoid a patch of ice. For a moment he considered returning to the house and apologizing. "But why should I?"

It had been a stupid row. They rarely argued, but when they eventually did, they fought like cats and dogs. But she was wrong this time. He *hadn't* opened up the doors on her advent calendar. Because if he had, he'd still have at least a handful of chocolates to his name, but he didn't.

And he'd *definitely* remember eating the chocolates and throwing the wrappers into the bin. "And I didn't."

Which begged the question, who did? As Percival glanced at a pig-head staring blankly through a butcher shop's window, he thought of Matilda. "It was her! She stitched me up!"

He cut through the market and headed for the back streets. The pavements were pure white, the snow billowy and completely undisturbed. Percival paused as a chilly breeze blew a swirl of powdery snow from the eaves of a nearby house. It glittered like pixie dust as it fell upon a bright red and blue box that sat upon the steps. The expressive vintage script and the picture on the label told Percival exactly what was inside. "I love firecrackers!" He looked around to see if he could find the box's owner, but the street was empty. Percival slid it open. Ten bright red firecrackers lay inside, each as long and thick as one of Uncle Florian's cigars. Percival twisted one of the black fuses between his fingers. He could almost hear their tiny voices and they were begging to be lit. A box of matches sat on the highest step. Percival reached for them, but stopped. "They're not mine," he mumbled. "And it's probably too early for that sort of noise anyway."

Perhaps he could come back later, and if the firecrackers were still unclaimed, it would be a sign he could have them. Percival nodded. That was the best plan. He walked away, failing to notice the livid scowling woman behind him, and the gleaming tusks that jutted from her lips.

He watched as a long icicle fell from the edge of a nearby roof. It struck the snow like a glassy dagger, and tumbled over, pointing to a fat golden brown apple strudel cooling on the windowsill, mere inches from Percival's fingers. He could almost taste the tart apple filling and the crisp buttery pastry. Percival's stomach rumbled. He'd left in such a hurry he'd forgotten breakfast. Leaning in to take a closer look, he noticed someone had even gone to the trouble of cutting the strudel into slices.

Perhaps he could take the smallest piece... "No," Percival muttered "it isn't mine". And thanks to Matilda, he knew exactly what it felt like to have someone steal a treat you were looking forward to.

He hurried away.

. . .

"This child can't be real!" Madam Grystle growled. The ice cream van followed behind at a leisurely pace, driven by Uffle and Gawp. "What's it going to take?" She closed her eyes and conjured another offering.

This one will surely tempt the confounded boy.

. . .

Percival picked up the heavy padded envelope sitting in the middle of the pavement. The top was open and a wad of bank notes almost spilled from it as he held it up. He'd never seen so much money.

"I better find out who this belongs to." Percival placed the envelope in his pocket and hurried on. The police station was only a few streets away.

. . .

Burning hot bile scorched Madam Grystle's throat. She swallowed it down and winced as it singed her windpipe. "I've never in my years known a more revolting child. What a disgusting, saintly beast." She thought about leaving this realm, of returning to her ice cavern and letting Krampus deal with this foolish pursuit on his own. But she shook her head with the same certainty as Percival had. She wasn't one for quitting and never had been.

Madam Grystle closed her eyes and forced her whirring mind to calm itself. The child was unbelievable, even now, he was taking the envelope of what he'd soon discover was fake money, to the police station. "Which means it's time to think outside the box.." Madam Grystle's cloud-like breath spilled from her mouth and nose and swirled down the street as she conjured her final offering.

. . .

Percival checked his coat pocket to make sure the envelope was still there. He hoped the police would find the owner, and quickly.

He almost reached the end of the peculiar street, where the residents must surely be the most trusting or careless people in the world, when he stopped. An old cigar box lay in the middle of the pavement. Inside it was a set of markers, and not the cheap kind Percival always used. No, these were made for artists and their ink was the most vivid and bright he'd ever seen.

"But they're not mine," Percival reminded himself. Except... except his eyes fell on one in particular. He was missing his purple marker and had spent days searching for it. Maybe he could just borrow this one, and return it later. "I'll only use it to color a couple of pages." He picked it up and slipped it into his pocket. "Just for now." Percival continued along the street.

"Hey!" Percival shouted as his hood was pulled down over his face and the world turned black. He squirmed as pointed fingers dug into his shoulder blades and held him in place. Percival jerked his head free. A woman stood before him. She wore thick wraparound sunglasses and tusks protruded from her crooked grin as she tightened her grip on his shoulders.

"Get off!" he cried as she pulled his hood down again.

"No." The woman's breath was rancid and made him think of dead things rotting on a beach. "I will not. You're a thief. A low down, rotten thief. And now you'll have to face your punishment!"

"Let me go!" As Percival struggled, the envelope fell from his pocket, scattering thin fake-looking money across the pavement. Something wriggled in his jacket. He screamed as the woman reached over to pull the marker from his pocket and a bright, glassy purple worm squirmed in her fingers before slithering across the ice into a nearby drain.

"Your ride awaits!" The woman spun Percival around to face the ice cream van that pulled up beside them. Two tiny men with fierce faces and wild black hair jumped down and threw the back of the van open. They reached inside, pulled out a burlap sack and raced towards Percival.

"Help!" Percival shouted. Everything turned black as the sack was plunged over his head. He screamed as their strong clawed hands lifted him up and carried him across the road. Percival winced as he was thrown onto a cold, hard floor. Then the doors slammed shut and the van sputtered to life.

The last thing Percival Greene heard before passing out was The Carol of the Bells playing with a discordant, funereal melody.

# CHAPTER SEVEN

It was at least an hour before Gabrielle realized Percival was missing. She'd assumed he was sulking in his room, but when she opened the door and saw he wasn't there, she grabbed her coat and ran out to look for him.

She checked the cake shop first because it was one of Percival's favorite places to daydream. A huge Christmas cake filled the window, it was covered with snowy frosting and a miniature steam train chugged around one of the tiers. There was no sign of Percival. The baker glanced at Gabrielle through the window and shook her head, then sternly pointed her finger and demanded that Gabrielle move along.

He wasn't outside the toy shop either, and the only footprints in the snow were hers.

She'd check the library.

Gabrielle set off down the back streets that served as a shortcut, keeping an eye out for his berry-red jacket as she went. She wasn't sure what she was going to do when she caught up with him. There would be words, and some of them would have to be strict, because he knew better than to run off on his own.

She was halfway down the road, when her right ear twinged, just as it always did when something was wrong with her brother. Then she noticed the trails of footprints with the star symbols in the heels.

Percival's boots.

They seemed light but then deeper in places where he'd presumably stopped. Beside them was a second pair of prints that were long and pointed. Gabrielle's gaze strayed to a single woven glove that lay among the muddled flurry of footprints that led toward the street. The ice glimmered in the compacted snow, it looked like someone had fallen there. Gabrielle picked the glove up.

It was Percival's.

Panic filled her heart as she scoured the street. She checked the line of terraced houses and caught a glimpse of an elderly woman with a thin, pinched face gazing back at her. The old lady began to step away from the window, but Gabrielle threw her hand up. "Please, help me!"

The old woman's lips drew into a firm line. She shook her head and gestured for Gabrielle to move along.

"Did you see what happened to my brother?" Gabrielle pressed.

The old lady opened the window. "Go now, or I'll call the police."

"Please, I need to find my brother. He's only nine!"

The old lady's face began to soften. She closed the window and a moment later, Gabrielle heard the sound of a lock turning. Her eyes smarted with tears. She wiped them away and stood taller.

The door opened and Gabrielle saw the odd dusty things that covered the wall inside. A wreath, red ribbons, silver bells, wooden crosses, and symbols written in chalk. The old lady peered out. "Come in," she said, her voice barely a rasp. "Quickly!"

The door jangled shut behind Gabrielle as she stepped into the warm hallway.

"This way," the old lady led Gabrielle into a kitchen overlooking the street. The air was thick with garlic and dozens of bulbs dangled from the ceiling and adorned the windowsill. Crosses and pentacles hung on the wall among strange symbols scrawled in charcoal.

"I use them to keep the Christmas devil away," the old lady explained.

*She's clearly mad.* Gabrielle just nodded as if it made perfect sense. "Sure. Look, I don't mean to be rude, but I need to find my brother. Did you see where he went?" She held up Percival's glove. "Did someone take him?"

"If that's your brother's glove then he's gone. Taken just like my own brother once was."

"Who took him? How long–"

The old lady placed a bony hand on Gabrielle's shoulder. "Calm down. He'll be back," she gave Gabrielle a bittersweet smile. "They only take them for a while."

"Who takes them?" Gabrielle felt sick. She clasped the edge of the sink.

"Krampus and his minions." The old lady's face turned ashen as she gazed through the window.

"Who is Krampus?" Gabrielle demanded. "Is he like those idiots trying to scare people in the market square? The ones dressed up like monsters?"

"No," the old lady shook her head. "He's nothing like them. Those people play at being Krampus, but Krampus doesn't play. He has the heart of a beast, and the guile of a toad. But he didn't take your brother himself. Madam

Grystle took him, her and Krampus's trolls. I saw it all."

"Madam Grystle?"

"She's an ogress. One of the worst. You can't miss her, tall as a ladder she is! With curved tusks, and eyes like a crocodile's. Her and the trolls put your brother in a sack and locked him up in an ice cream van. And then they drove away."

"An ice cream van!" Gabrielle shivered as she recalled the same vehicle parked near her uncle's house and the creepy woman at the window in the middle of the night. She'd convinced herself it was nothing but a half-dream. A nightmare. "I don't believe in trolls and-"

"You don't have to believe in Krampus, but he believes in you. He and his trolls come for the bad ones. They took my brother too, many, many years ago. My brother forgot, but I didn't. It happened one Krampusnight, over sixty years ago. I saw Krampus himself, he put Jakob in a burlap sack and carried him away on his sleigh. And when he brought him back, Jakob was silent, broken and covered in soot like he'd just come down a chimney. And I'll always remember the look in his eyes. Like he was somewhere else, some place far away. He never spoke of that night, not once. But I'll never forget, never."

"Where did they take your brother?"

"Off to the dark lands, to punish him. Krampus punishes all the wrongdoers, you see, and Jakob was always getting into trouble. Until that night at least. Because after his run-in with Krampus, he took to goodness with an abandon that would shame a saint."

"Look, I'm sorry but this story is really hard to believe. I just need to find Percival. Can I use your phone? I need to call the police."

"The police won't help," the old lady said. "They know

what goes on, and they keep themselves to themselves." Her smile turned bittersweet. "Everyone knows what happens on Krampusnight. No one talks about it, but they all know. I've said too much myself. It's time for you to go, but I wish you luck in finding your brother. He'll come back, I promise. Once he's been punished." The old lady ushered Gabrielle from the kitchen.

"Please!" Gabrielle said. "Just tell me where he is."

The old lady sighed. "Well, I suppose it's too late for me now, anyway. I've told you most of Krampus's tale and he'll come calling if that's his will. And neither wards or garlic will stop him once he's been wronged. You want to find Krampus, yes?"

"If that's where Percival is."

"Go to the catacombs. That's where they take them, or so it's said."

"The catacombs?"

"They're on the edge of the city. By the lake. No one goes there, not even the police. There's something down there. A dragon, or a monster. We hear its roar every December and smoke rises up from the ground. Go there. That's where the beast of Christmas comes from."

# CHAPTER EIGHT

To Gabrielle, the lake looked just like one of the baker's Christmas cakes; vast and round and the snow gleamed upon its surface like sugar crystals. She kicked frozen pebbles and shards of ice as she walked around the shoreline clutching Percival glove. "I'll find you, Perce!" she promised as her breath puffed from her mouth like gusts of steam.

A small building with a portico and sloped roof stood near the water's edge and Gabrielle could see a group of teenagers sitting on the stone wall that surrounded it. They all wore dark clothing. Black coats, shirts, sweaters, trousers and pointy leather shoes. Silver rings gleamed in their noses and eyebrows. They made Gabrielle think of ravens, sitting and conspiring dark, secret plans. They glanced up as she approached and muttered in low voices.

Gabrielle ignored them as she headed toward the iron gates that barred a flight of steps and tunnel leading under the building. A sign had been mounted on the gates, but she couldn't understand it, other than one word *mort.*

Death.

Gabrielle suppressed a shiver.

One of the girls called to her.

"I can't understand you," Gabrielle said. "Do you speak English?"

The girl flicked back her long black hair. "Are you lost?"

"No. Why, are you?" Gabrielle instantly regretted her waspish tone.

"What are you here for, little girl?" The tall boy beside the girl asked. "The catacombs are shut. And anyway, they're too scary for you."

"I'm not scared of anything, apart from being bored to death." Gabrielle glanced from the fearsome silver bone threaded through his pierced nose to his icy blue eyes.

"Oooh!" the boy held up his hands. "I'm so sorry!" All of them, apart from the girl, laughed at this. Gabrielle ignored them as she looked up the hill, toward the parking lot, and noticed the battered old ice cream van.

"Are you looking for someone?" the girl asked.

"My brother." Gabrielle pulled the glove from her pocket. "He might have been wearing a glove like this. And a red jacket. Someone told me there were men with him. Little men."

"Gnomes?" the boy with the nose ring asked. He laughed and fixed Gabrielle with a withering look.

"Leave her alone, Dieter." The girl jumped from the wall and approached Gabrielle. "I'm Emmeline, by the way. And no, we haven't seen any boys. Or little men."

"They might have gone in there." Gabrielle nodded to the tunnel.

"No one went in there. Not in the last hour," Emmeline said.

"How do I get in?" Gabrielle nodded to the tunnel entrance.

"You don't want to go in there, little girl," Dieter said. "That's the entrance to the underworld!"

Emmeline tutted. "No it's not. But he's right, you shouldn't go. The tunnels are deep and...there's things. Weird stuff."

"Have you ever been in there?" Gabrielle asked.

"Of course," Emmeline said. "But not far."

"She's frightened of the tunnels," Dieter said. "I've been in, right to the end. It's nothing."

"How did you get in?" Gabrielle asked.

"I picked the lock," Dieter said. "It's easy." He pulled a long pin from his pocket.

"Could you pick it again?" Gabrielle asked. "I've got to find my brother. Someone said that's where they took him."

"I think you should call the police," Emmeline said.

"Once we've gone," one of the boys on the wall added.

"I don't have time. Listen," Gabrielle said to Dieter, "I'll pay you if you open the gate and take me through the tunnels. Or if you're too scared, just let me in."

"How much?" Dieter jumped from the wall and towered over Gabrielle.

Gabrielle routed through her pocket and pulled out a couple of crumpled notes.

Emmeline closed Gabrielle's hand over her money, before turning on Dieter. "You're not taking her money. Just let her in. Right?"

Dieter's nose ring made him look even more bullish as he frowned. Finally he exhaled, giving a long, loud sigh. "You want to go to into the underworld, little girl? Then we'll take you into the underworld."

# CHAPTER NINE

Dieter slipped the pin into the lock. There was a loud click and the gates swung open. He gave Gabrielle a theatrical bow and ushered her through. Gabrielle rolled her eyes as she strode past him.

The air was thick with must and damp. An old kiosk stood in the shadows, its rusty metal shutter drawn and locked. The tunnel loomed like a backdrop; beyond the first few feet there was nothing but pure darkness. "Has anyone got a light?" Gabrielle asked with as much nonchalance as she could muster.

"You're badly prepared for your journey into Hades, little girl." Dieter flicked a switch on his phone and a beam of light shone around them. "Now, let's see how brave you really are. How about a bet? You make it to the end of the tunnel and I won't ask for the money Emmeline told you you could keep. But if you don't, you give me double. Yes?"

"Dieter!" Emmeline said.

"Deal," Gabrielle shook his hand. His grip was tight, but she refused to wince. At least she'd have company now, and light. The others switched their phones on and the light played across the floor and ceiling. The limestone walls were slick. Cold water dripped from above and the smell of must grew stronger the further down the tunnel they went. "What's this place for?" Gabrielle's voice echoed around her.

"What do you think?" Dieter held his flashlight beneath his chin. "It's where they bury the dead."

"That was a long time ago," Emmeline added. "Look, there's nothing to find here. If someone told you that your brother came here, they were joking." She seemed uneasy as she gazed back to the distant circle of daylight.

"I need to make sure." Gabrielle's ear twitched again. Percival was close, and he was in danger. They turned a bend and the tunnel divided into two forks. "Right or left?"

"Left's the devil's path," Dieter said. "So that's-"

A shrill squeal echoed down the tunnel, like a giant kettle whistling from the very center of the earth. Gabrielle shivered and the hairs on the nape of her neck bristled.

"I'm going back," said one of the boys, his voice shaky. The rest of the group agreed and turned to follow him.

Dieter cursed but they just ignored him and kept going.

"What was that noise?" Gabrielle asked.

"The dragon," Dieter said. "Hopefully we won't have to deal with it." He smiled, but there was a nervous gleam in his eyes. "Unless you want to go back too."

"I've got to find my brother." Gabrielle marched along the passage to the right. Soon the lights from Dieter and Emmeline's phones caught up with her. Something lay in the middle of the stony floor, splayed like a great big spider. "Shine your lights there," Gabrielle pointed to the ground. "Please."

Emmeline jumped as the light hit the spider-like form.

"It's Percy's glove!" Gabrielle snatched it up.

"Percy?" Emmeline asked.

"My brother." Gabrielle pulled the other glove from her pocket and held them together. "I told you he was down here!" She continued along the passage, but Dieter and Emmeline paused. "Are you coming?" Gabrielle asked.

"We don't go down there." Dieter pointed the light past Gabrielle to a series of steps descending into the darkness.

"Why?"

"We just don't," Dieter said.

"You dared me, remember? What's the problem? Are you scared?" Gabrielle's words flew from her lips in puffs of steam.

Dieter shook his head. "No."

"I am," Emmeline said. "Come on, let's go back and I'll call the police as soon as I get reception on my phone."

"There's no time," Gabrielle insisted. "Come on, hurry!"

"No." Dieter folded his arms. "We tried to go down there before...and we turned back."

"Why?"

"That's where the noises came from." Emmeline said. "The howling. And that horrible black smoke. It burnt our throats."

Gabrielle rolled her eyes. Despite their fearsome appearances they were just as timid as Percival. "Just lend me your phone so I can see where I'm going. I'll give it back as soon as I'm done looking. I promise."

Emmeline held her phone out, but the light flickered. She examined the screen. "It's nearly out of charge. Dieter, give her yours."

"No."

"Fine!" Gabrielle stepped toward the stairs, inching her

hand along the wall to find her way. Her heart thumped hard as she peered blindly into the darkness ahead.

*What am I doing?* Gabrielle wondered.

The others muttered behind her. She crossed her fingers they'd follow.

Finally she heard their footsteps and the eerie blue light of Deiter's phone played across the wall. Gabrielle recoiled as something fat, black and many-legged scuttled away from her fingers.

"I set the timer for five minutes." Dieter's voice was sulky and childish. "When it goes off, I'm going back. With or without you."

Gabrielle continued down the stairs, they seemed as if they were going on for forever. She wanted to call out for Percival, but the thought of raising her voice sent a shiver of dread through her. What if someone else heard...

The stairs ended in a passage with a dim circle of murky light glowing in the distance. "What's that?" Gabrielle asked.

"I don't know..." Dieter said. As they walked toward the light, the din rang out again. It was almost deafening as it screeched and echoed along the narrow tunnel, followed by a cloud of steam and an acrid stench.

"Dragon smoke!" Dieter began to back away.

"It's not smoke. It's steam." Gabrielle batted it from her face and hurried on. "Come on."

"No way!"

Gabrielle turned to find Dieter hurrying back toward the stairs. As the light from his phone receded Emmeline reached a hand out for Gabrielle. "Come with us. We'll call the police, I promise."

"I'm not going with you. I have to find my brother."

Emmeline tried to grab her, but Gabrielle wriggled from her grasp and ran down the corridor toward the eerie fiery light.

"Come back!" Emmeline called.

"Go," Gabrielle shouted, as the squealing din rose again. "And thanks for your help." She ran, her heart thumping hard. "You better be here, Percival Greene."

A pointed arch marked the end of the corridor and a red and orange glow flickered in the huge chamber beyond. Burning torches jutted from sconces, throwing their light upon the tall pillars that stretched up toward the sooty black ceiling.

A droning growl rang out and Gabrielle stopped dead in her tracks as she saw the source of the noise and smoke.

# CHAPTER
# TEN

A steam train, with four long rail carriages that were as black as coal, chugged in the center of the cavern. Two metallic silver horns jutted from its cab, reaching out over the front of the engine and a slash of red paint formed a devilish grin.

The train whistled, making Gabrielle jump, as steam belched from its chimney and billowed up to the cavern's sooty black ceiling. Then the door of the front carriage flew open and a little man in a duffel coat jumped down. Wisps of wiry black hair poked out from under his hood, framing his pale face and hooked nose. Another man followed, wearing a pair of goggles that obscured most of his soot streaked face. They began to argue in a strange, jabbering dialect, then one of them stalked away and the other rushed after him. They vanished through a door in the cavern wall, slamming it behind them with a solid thump.

Silence fell. Gabrielle caught her breath as she walked along the side of the dark shadowy train, determined to find Percival. She crept up the steps of the first carriage. It was still and quiet. Old fashioned polished brass rails and empty luggage racks hung from the dark wood paneled ceiling. Plush red velvet upholstery lined the elaborately carved rows of empty benches. She hurried back to the platform and peered into the next car, it was empty too. As she headed toward the third she heard muffled cries and thumps and followed the din to the dark windowless carriage at the end of the train. She placed her ear up to the wall. Tiny voices cried out, begging to be released.

"Percy?" Gabrielle whispered as loudly as she dared. "Is that you?"

Several anxious voices replied, creating a discordant jumble of squeals and yelps.

"Percival?" Gabrielle called. "Are you in there?"

"Gabby?"

"Yes, it's me. Hang on, I'll find a way to get you out." Gabrielle ran back to the door of the third carriage and bound up the stairs. It had the same dark wood interior as the other carriage but paneled walls divided the space into six private compartments. Each of the rooms had glass windows that overlooked the long aisle that ran down the middle of the car and at the far end she spotted the door that connected the two carriages.

It was locked. Gabrielle looked around, searching for something to force the door open with. There was nothing, so she tried the first compartment but it was also locked. She shoved the door of the second compartment and it flew open. As she searched the room, a low clanking sound rang out through the chamber. Gabrielle crouched at the window and watched as the two little men emerged from their door and hurried across the cavern.

A pair of double doors slid open in the far wall and the tall woman in the scarlet coat emerged from what looked like an elevator. It was the same woman Gabrielle had seen driving an ice cream van at midnight. She strode into the cavern, followed by three pairs of little men in duffel coats. Each pair carried wriggling burlap sacks between them as they headed straight toward the carriage.

Gabrielle ducked down, scooted across the floor and kicked the door of her compartment shut. Her heart raced as she switched off the light and carefully reached up to pull down the window shades.

The woman jangled a set of keys as she walked down the aisle and unlocked the door to the windowless carriage where Percy was. Peering carefully through a crack at the edge of the compartment window, Gabrielle could see a long room filled with wooden racks and upon each shelf there was a squirming sack.

Gabrielle ducked low as the horde of little men shuffled past her door, and she watched as they loaded the sacks onto the railcar. The woman waited until they'd stowed the last one, then she slammed the door shut and locked it.

"Go," She barked at one of them. "Tell the engine driver to make haste. We have much distance to cover." She sniffed the air and a slow grin passed across her pale white face. "And Krampus awaits his special gift."

The man gazed up at her, as if entranced by her hideous tusks.

"Move, troll! Run, creep, crawl. Go!" The woman clapped her hands.

*Troll. Krampus.* Gabrielle swallowed. It was real. This woman must be the ogress. *Madam Grystle.*

Gabrielle watched in horror as Madam Grystle unlocked the compartment right next door and ushered the trolls inside. A shrill whistle echoed across the cavern walls and the train juddered. Gabrielle sprang to her feet, slipped out of her hiding place and rushed down the aisle of the carriage toward the platform.

She stumbled on a step and grabbed the door handle. It writhed, silver and snakelike, then the lock popped down with a clunk. She gasped as it hissed at her, before coiling around on itself and settling into the dark wooden panel.

With a loud groan, the train rattled itself to life and her heart raced as the carriage began to move.

# CHAPTER
# ELEVEN

The train wheezed like an ancient giant. Wreaths of steam filled the air obscuring the platform, the cavern, and the very world itself. As if they were lost in some great, terrible fog. A shrill whistle echoed across the platform as the train rolled back and came to a stop. A loud grinding clank rang out from the front of the train and it lurched forward, its wheels clicking and clacking upon the rails.

The train sped forward and another whistle rang out, followed by a dirge-like bellow. Gabrielle ran to a window and slid it open. All she could see was the black pitted, jagged rock that lined the tunnel. She stole a deep breath and tried to contain her rising panic.

Where was the train going? She imagined it taking her down into the belly of the earth. For where else would Krampus live?

Her claustrophobia swelled up as the train rattled and clanked further and further into the darkness, before finally breaking out into blinding light.

Gabrielle shielded her eyes against the harsh glare, and as they adjusted she tried to peek through her fingers. Snowy fields surrounded the train and in the distance, the city spires and towers grew smaller and smaller.

The train thundered towards the surrounding hills and mountains while a pack of dogs bounded through the snow, keeping pace with Gabrielle's carriage. Were they dogs, or wolves? Their mournful howls rose above the clacking wheels of the train, as if warning Gabrielle to get off. That this was her last chance.

But it was too late. She was locked in.

She tiptoed back to her compartment and watched as the setting sun turned smoky red and the mountains glittered in shades of salmon pink and glacier blue. Pine trees towered over the tracks and wood smoke coiled up from the chimneys of a distant wooden lodge. Gabrielle wondered if the people inside could see the train, and if they knew about the sinister cargo it contained.

They passed signposts, their words and letters different to the ones in the city. She wasn't sure but they seemed to be written in some strange, new language. The words on the final post became legible as Gabrielle attempted to read them:

*'Welcome to the Dark Lands.'*

The train swept over a viaduct. An icy river weaved its way through the land far below as they rattled and chugged toward a range of high jagged mountains. Sheer stone cliffs rose up around the train, like walls, blocking out the last of the dying light.

Great drifts of snow teetered high upon the grey granite and weighed down the branches of the withered frostbitten trees.

"I've got to break Percival out, and get us off the train!" Gabrielle whispered. She opened the door and checked the aisle. Light spilled from the first compartment, illuminating the locked carriage door. Gabrielle tip-toed towards it, her heart beating hard as shrill, excited laughter rattled the glass and ominous silhouettes flickered upon the walls. She took a deep breath and craned her neck as she peered through the compartment window.

Madam Grystle sat on a plush bench, her sunglasses glinting on the red cushion beside her. As the ogress blinked, her eyes were covered in milky white films. Like a bird. Or a crocodile. Her tusks jutted proudly from her lips as she held out a brown paper bag and shook it, taunting the trolls that sat before her. They watched intently as she unwrapped inky black sweets from the bag and threw them up into the air. The trolls caught them with the ruthless snapping efficiency of dogs. Then they licked their lips with their dark candy stained tongues, leaving blue and black streaks all around their mouths.

The train whistled and one of the slobbering trolls turned towards Gabrielle. She ducked down. Had it seen her?

A hefty thump rattled the floor and she heard muffled footsteps coming towards her. Gabrielle scurried down the corridor. Her legs felt hollow as she opened her compartment door and slipped inside. She pulled it closed with trembling fingers, and her heart raced as she listened to each steady, intent footstep of the troll as it clomped down the aisle towards her hiding place.

# CHAPTER TWELVE

Gabrielle scrambled up into the luggage rack and lay flat. She pressed her face into the mesh and willed her body to be completely still.

The compartment door slid open and the troll stomped in. It sniffed the air, its piggy eyed gaze sweeping over the compartment. "Child?" it gurgled.

The windows turned black as the train swept into a tunnel but Gabrielle could still see the dark silhouette of troll amid the light filtering from the next compartment. It reached up with its grubby fingers and flicked the light switch but the compartment remained dark.

The missing lightbulb was still warm where it lay safely tucked in Gabrielle's pocket.

The troll tromped into the middle of the compartment and muttered, its voice clipped and guttural.

*It can smell me!*

The corridor lit up with a flash of green light, and a chorus of cackles and giggles rang out, followed by what sounded like the patter of candy tumbling onto the carriage floor. The troll muttered again, spun around on its pointy shoes and left, slamming the door shut behind him.

Gabrielle remained quiet and still until she heard it rejoin the others, then she climbed onto the seat below to think things through.

There was no way of getting to Percival without the trolls or Madam Grystle seeing her.

"How am I going to get him out?" Gabrielle whispered, wishing she'd asked to borrow Dieter's lock pick. Not that he would have given it to her, or that she'd know how to use it.

An eerie light flooded the train as it emerged from the tunnel into a vast snowy expanse, quite unlike anything she had ever seen.

The dark blue sky was shot through with glimmering stars and a bright crescent moon while intermittent waves of bottle-green light danced among them, giving the scattered clouds an unearthly glow. The land seemed to stretch out forever, a sea of china white peppered with wooded hills. Lights twinkled here and there, reminding Gabrielle of faerie lanterns flitting through an enchanted eve.

As beautiful as the place was, she felt uneasy because there was also something sinister about it. The forests were dark, darker than they had any reason to be, their shadows as deep and black as raven feathers.

Gabrielle gasped as they passed a gathering of snowmen that had been arranged into a strange tableau. Several had missing limbs, while others had far too many and some had long wavy tentacles that weaved and reached through the frosty air. A snow woman sat above them on a grey polished granite throne. Her head was capped with a jagged icicle crown and her flint eyes were deep and cruel. Then the train veered away, speeding toward a dark mountain that rose in the distance. Soon it filled the horizon, its shape resembling an animal-like head crowned with great arching horns.

The mountain passed from view as the train swept around a sharp bend, and raced alongside a frozen river. Steam flitted past the window like scraps of cloud and red lights flashed as the train slowly approached a depot. Gleaming icicles hung from the high pointed roof of the station house, its narrow eye-like windows looking down upon the crowd that waited on the platform.

Gabrielle flinched as she looked closer, each figure was utterly nightmarish. She spotted a rotund man with the thicket of wild red hair and pale yellow tusks. Beside him stood three ladies, their tails flicking below the hems of their neat olive green coats. A little girl waited beside them in a pretty icy blue dress and Gabrielle gasped as her jet black eyes flashed above her miserly sneer.

A huge bear ran across the snow field, toward the platform. It was wearing russet trousers under a black tunic and the sack it carried left a coppery-red trail in the snow.

The carved wooden sign post above the station read:

"Little Nowhere upon the Sleet."

The train stopped and Gabrielle ducked down in case any of the creatures came her way, but the crowd gathered around the two empty carriages and quickly climbed aboard. Then a shrill whistle rang out, and the train was off.

It passed several odd little villages and finally came to a stop at a station with a sign that read:

"Hazelby-upon-Krampus"

The carriage door rattled as the silver snake-like handles hissed and unfurled. Madam Grystle strolled into the corridor, unlocked the adjoining door and watched as her trolls waddled inside and began to drag the sacks out.

Terrified cries filled the corridor. Gabrielle hands curled into fists and she winced as her nails bit into her palms. She had to stop herself from bursting through the compartment door and shoving the trolls head first into the snow. There were too many of them, not to mention the ogress and the other beasts on the train too.

She watched in silent frustration as the trolls manhandled the sacks, tossing them out into the billowy snow. Sleds pulled by great grey deerhounds paused alongside the tracks. Ragged puffs of steam burst from their excited maws as they scratched the icy ground.

The sled drivers wore dark fur coats and towering hats. They stared ahead impassively while the trolls piled the writhing sacks upon the sleds. As soon as a sled was filled, the driver would crack his whips and tugged the reins, the hounds bellowing as they reared up and raced away, churning the snow as if it were little more than confetti.

Gabrielle turned back toward the door and peeked out from behind the window shade. Two trolls emerged into the corridor with a black wooly sack wrapped with a great big red ribbon.

Madam Grystle followed closely behind them, a trace of a smile on her crooked lips as she sniffed the air. Gabrielle shivered, as the ogress's eyes flickered toward her compartment. She paused there for a moment, clasped her hands together and pranced toward the exit, stepping gracefully down into the snow, followed by the rest of her trolls. Gabrielle watched them secure the woolen sack to the top of a horse-drawn sleigh, its red ribbon fluttering in the chilly air as a muffled scream issued from the sack. "Gabrielle!"

Gabrielle scrambled out into the corridor and leapt for the door handle just as the whistle sounded. The locks popped down as the handles hissed and writhed like silver snakes. "No!" She pounded her fists upon the window, but the door was locked tight.

The train shook and rumbled as it drew away. Gabrielle watched the horses galloping through the snow, carrying Percival further and further away.

# CHAPTER THIRTEEN

"I've got to get off!" Gabrielle ran down the corridor, pulling at the locked doors and banging on the windows. The rattle and clang of the engine was thunderous, and wisps of steam flew past the carriage. Gabrielle shoved at the last door, tears of frustration stinging her eyes. She wiped them away and forced herself to take a deep breath.

Branches thwacked against the glass. The train was speeding thorough a forest. Gabrielle frantically searched for a way out and spotted a hatch in the roof. She needed a ladder. She looked all around, and leapt toward the dark narrow wooden door marked storeroom.

It was unlocked. Twisted black and white striped wrappers littered the floor and the smell of licorice and coal dust filled the air. Crates of the sweets were stacked high in the corner. Gabrielle grabbed the boxes one by one and stacked them under the hatch, until it was high enough for her to reach.

She scampered to the top and pulled at the lever until a blast of icy wind bit into her fingers and the hatch flew open. Gabrielle pulled herself up onto the frosty roof fighting to keep her balance as the towering pine trees whipped past. Through the branches she could see a village of strange, conical buildings. Warm yellow light spilled from the windows but the houses looked stark and sinister.

She clung to the edge of the hatch as the train rumbled along, ducking down as the low branches shot toward her. A sharp crack and the brush of cold needles broke her grip and swept her along the rooftop. Gabrielle threw out a hand to grab hold of the guardrail but it was too late.

"No!" She screamed as she tumbled from the roof into a void of white.

# CHAPTER FOURTEEN

Everything was white and silent, save for the train's distant receding clatter. The bank of snow was deep and as soft as a pillow but Gabrielle gasped as cold chunks of it tumbled down upon her. She tried to pull herself up but her hands came away icy and wet. She shifted onto her knees, and then her feet and pushed herself up until her head and shoulders broke through the snow.

She struggled through deep drifts until she reached the slope where the track lay. Gabrielle leaned low as she climbed and thrust out her hands to grab at stray roots.

When she reached the train tracks and the icy path beside them she stopped to shake the snow from her coat. Then she hung it upon a branch while she brushed away the remaining snow from her clothes. Percy's gloves were too small to wear, so she put them back in her pocket and rubbed her hands together, trying to fight the spreading numbness.

Taking a deep breath, Gabrielle put her coat back on, stamped her shoes and continued along the track.

The further she walked, the larger the great horned mountain grew as it loomed above the tree line.

Gabrielle slowed as she approached the gleaming lights of the cone shaped houses in the dale below. They formed a ragged circle around a huge bonfire. Trolls wandered about, their shouts high and feral as they added logs and branches to the smoky sizzling pyre. Gabrielle backed away from the rise, concerned they might spot her as she made her way along the track.

It felt like a landscape from a dream or a nightmare. Yet the bite of the wind was real enough, and so was the crunch of snow beneath her shoes. Green lights flashed across the sky, a magical, yet eerie sight.

A branch creaked behind her and Gabrielle came to a halt. She glanced around and spotted a blackbird watching from a snow laden branch. "I don't like the way you're looking at me," she mumbled, before hurrying on.

. . .

It felt as if she'd been walking for hours but her watch indicated it had only been a few minutes. The tiny images of the sun and moon held fast to their positions in the sky. If they were moving, they were doing so incredibly slowly. She shook her wrist and tapped on the glass. Perhaps time passed differently here.

Gabrielle glanced back. She'd definitely made good progress and the mountain ahead was much closer now. She could see all of the terrible intricate details of the beastly head that had been hewn from the majestic peak. The arching horns had grown so large they seemed to pierce the very sky.

The tracks were beginning to veer away, if she was going to get to the mountain she'd have to forge her own path. The stone ballast under the tracks sloped down to a wide swathe of snow and at the far side there was a little forest. The trees were small and as black as coal, save for tiny lights that twinkled like Christmas bulbs. There was something odd and troubling about it, but there was no other way, not if she wanted to reach the mountain.

Gabrielle clutched Percival's glove as she climbed down the rocky slope and waded across the pristine snow filled meadow.

. . .

Soon the forest stood before Gabrielle, its bushy trees only a few heads taller than her own. They were Christmas trees, their dark branches covered with drab olive-green needles, their tips as black as soot. Tiny colorless baubles hung from their branches, their surfaces tarnished and pitted. Silvery scarlet foil flitted in the breeze, giving a halfhearted sparkle as it peeled away from the rusting buckets that held the trees upright.

Wind stirred from the east and the branches rustled together, creating an eerie noise like muffled harps. Like harps being played under the sea. Gabrielle shivered as she imagined spindly limbed Sirens plucking strings, their ashen faces gazing up from deep below the waves.

She glanced back toward the tracks. Perhaps she could...

Gabrielle froze.

Someone was standing upon the crest, watching her.

Then they slipped back and vanished among the trunks of the pine trees.

Gabrielle plunged into the forest. "If I keep going straight I'll be out the other side in no time."

She often found talking to herself helped when she was frightened.

It didn't this time.

# CHAPTER
# FIFTEEN

As Gabrielle parted the branches the little baubles hanging from them lit up, illuminating the murky thicket beyond. While it was good to see where she was going, it meant anyone else in the forest could see where she was too. The realization made her shiver, but there was nothing to do except press on.

The space between trees grew wider and it soon became easier to walk without setting off the lights. The scent of pine tickled her nose as she ventured deeper into the forest. When she glanced back she could barely see the train tracks or the snowy land beyond.

There were just trees, endless stumpy trees all around her.

And then she heard a crash of branches from somewhere ahead.

Gabrielle froze, listening carefully as the odd harp-like sound of the branches played and light flashed in the gloom.

It winked out.

She stood still and gazed into the murk.

Was that someone standing ahead, waiting near the small cluster of trees?

Gabrielle walked slowly, keeping away from the baubles that hung from the branches lest they give her position away.

"Stop!" The voice was little more than a hiss.

Gabrielle darted away and screamed as she collided with a small, crooked figure. It was a troll. He gazed at her with bone white eyes that shone below his tangle of black wiry hair, then he raised a stumpy finger to his lips. "Shhh!"

Before she could respond he clamped his grey grimy sleeve over her mouth. It reeked of coal dust and earth, and other things she'd sooner not consider.

"Don't speak," he said. "Just give me your coat. Quickly!"

Gabrielle shook her head. "It's freezing cold, and you've already got a coat-"

"I need something new to wear. Before it gets me." His eyes burned with fear as he gazed around the trees.

"What will get you?"

"Jólakötturinn!"

"A what??"

"The Christmas Cat! If he finds me and I don't have new clothes, he'll eat me. He's been stalking me for hours!" The troll's eyes hardened. "Give me that coat, or I'll-"

"What?" Gabrielle bunched her hands into fists. The trolls were fearsome, but less so when there was only one of them.

"I'll...I'll choke you!" His sinewy hands reached for her and Gabrielle had no doubt he'd do what he threatened. She sidestepped his reach and pulled his long wiry beard. The troll howled and flailed, crashing into a nearby tree. A cluster of baubles shone and glistened all around them.

Gabrielle's breath caught in her throat.

A huge cat crouched at the edge of the darkness, watching. It was as big as a panther, with black, grey and blue striped fur. Its wild green eyes flickered and its whiskers stood out like the bristles of a broom as it grinned with needle-like teeth. It stalked toward them on monstrous paws, its long tail twitching.

"Get back!" The troll growled at the cat. He pulled an ax from his coat and swung it around.

The cat leaped, setting off a string of baubles as it landed before them. It batted the ax from the troll's quivering hand with a single swipe and stamped it into the snow.

"Take this, wrap it around your neck. It can't attack you if you're wearing new clothes." A hoarse, female voice whispered from the darkness and a thick grey scarf fell like a wooly serpent around Gabrielle's neck.

She pulled it tight as the monstrous cat bore down upon her. It growled and sniffed the air. "Take that off" it said with a deep, regal growl.

"Why?" Gabrielle was determined to show no fear. Or at least as little as she could.

"Because I said so."

"What would happen if I did?" Gabrielle knotted the scarf tighter.

"I'd put you out of your misery." The cat's voice was as smooth as silk. "By swallowing you whole."

"No, I don't think I'd like that. I think I'll keep my new scarf."

The cat gave Gabrielle a look of deep disappointment as it added, "Then go!"

Gabrielle backed away as the cat advanced upon the troll. "You on the other paw, have nothing new to wear," the cat said. "So you will be my next feast. Perhaps there'll even be enough bones and sinew left to make a stock for my Christmas Day pie."

"No!" the troll dug the ax from the snow and fled into the trees.

"And so the hunt continues," the cat said to Gabrielle. "But my, I would have enjoyed a snack." It gave a low desolate yawn, swished its long striped tail, gave Gabrielle a crestfallen look and slunk into the gloom.

Gabrielle plunged through the forest, glancing back every now and then to ensure she wasn't being followed. For she'd never known a cat that could be trusted.

Finally, she broke from the trees. The mountain towered above her, the huge horns jutting from the jagged edifice. Gabrielle trudged through the vast dark shadows that they cast upon the snow, and made her way toward the enormous doorway at the foot of the mountain.

. . .

A giant swirling 'K' was carved into the great wooden doors and elaborate barbed brambles sprouted from the top of the letter encircling it like a wreath.

Three stone trolls stood on each side of the entrance. They stared out at Gabrielle with sightless eyes, their teeth drawn into savage grins. Each of them clutched a cudgel, and the tallest one carried a sack along with a low, cunning look.

"What do I do now?" Clearly, knocking on the doors wasn't an option. "I wonder if they are locked?" She reached up to push them, and a deep cracking sound split the air around her. Gabrielle flinched, expecting to find rocks raining down from the mountain, but the din came from the statues. Chunks of stone slid from their faces and limbs, and fell into the snow. Their eyes sparkled and they gave fiendish grins as they came to life.

"We're so glad you've finally made it!" a hoarse voice cried from behind her. Madam Grystle emerged from the forest, plucking pine needles from her long coat. "That scarf suits you, but it didn't suit Jólakötturinn. Indeed, it deprived him of his feast. I risked my life to enter that forest and save you, which leaves you in my debt. I don't want much in return, just a simple answer. Tell me, how did you evade us on Krampusnight?"

"I don't know what you're talking about. I just want to find my brother and-"

"I asked you a question and I demand an answer. Our spies told us of the wicked crimes you've committed all over the city. It was a most impressive list, but neither I, nor the great Krampus himself could snag you. How did you manage it? What magic did you wield?"

Gabrielle kept her silence. She had no idea what the ogress was talking about, but trying to explain that to her wouldn't be of any use.

"Very well. I'll discover the nature of your sorcery sooner or later." Madam Grystle turned to the trolls. "Clamp her in irons to contain her magic."

One of the trolls grinned as it pulled a pair of manacles from a sack. The others raised their cudgels, daring Gabrielle to fight back but she knew when she was outnumbered. The grinning troll closed in, snapping the manacles around her feet and snickering as he locked them in place. "The witch is contained!" it announced in a high, rasping voice.

"Yes, she is." Madam Grystle clapped her hands. "And where should we take her?" she asked, with an expectant smile.

"Down, down, down! Down with wicked vile clowns," one of the trolls uttered. The others joined in, "Down, down, down, to the depths of Krampus town!"

Gabrielle refused to scream as they lifted her and carried

her away from the doors. They stood facing the sheer grey side of the mountain and one of the trolls rapped its knuckles upon the rock. A hidden door slid open revealing a corridor lined with flaming torches. The trolls hoisted her up as if she were nothing more than a sack of potatoes and the click of Madam Grystle's shoes followed behind them.

Two mine carts waited at the end of the corridor and a stretch of track descended into the darkness. "Let me go!" Gabrielle demanded. She squirmed but they held her firm.

"As you ask, so you get," one of the trolls said. Then they dropped her into the cart with a heavy clang. Gabrielle tried to climb out, but one of them pushed her back as the other pulled a handle and fixed her with a savage grin. "Down, down, down, to the depths of Krampus town!"

The mine cart lurched forward, sweeping her away as it plunged down into the great black void.

# CHAPTER
# SIXTEEN

The cart flew down the tracks at breakneck speed and sparks burst from the wheels as it rocked to and fro upon the rails.

The heavy smell of coal rose up on a blast of hot air and dim red light glowed in the deep fissures and danced along the walls, illuminating clusters of stalactites.

Gabrielle ducked as they whizzed past like hanging stone daggers, then peered over the front of the cart.

The rusty track spanned a deep gorge, and below it were pools of fiery red bubbling lava. The ceiling rose away and the cart turned a corner, tilting crazily over the track. "No!" Gabrielle's words were snatched from her mouth as she shot around a hairpin turn and the tracks swept down past the sweltering pools of molten rock into a dark tunnel.

Something roared in the gloom, the sound distant and yet close enough to freeze her blood. She pried at the manacles around her legs, but they were stuck firm.

And then the cart slowed, screeching to a stop.

Gabrielle peered down over the side, into the vast cavern below. It was lit by blazing torches and tiny figures moved across the floor. It took Gabrielle a moment to realize they were children, tethered to each other by lengths of chain. Trolls stood sentry, overseeing them as they toiled in the hot sweaty cavern. Some scrubbed the broad floor with giant toothbrushes, others pulled stringy black hairs from enormous drains. Along one wall, dozens of children formed a line around a colossal sink, scrubbing the huge piles of dishes that soaked in the grey greasy water.

A fleet of sleds filled the other side of the cavern. Kids kneeled before them, cleaning and polishing the frames and runners. Others tended to a pack of wolves, clipping their toenails and grooming their fur with hair-mangled brushes.

The children worked in silence. They kept their heads down, and adopted postures of resignation and despair.

Gabrielle had never seen anything so miserable in her life and her fury eclipsed her fear.

As she stood up to protest but her bound feet sent her tumbling back onto her rear end.

The cart creaked and rumbled, plunging down the track into a narrow passage lined with glowing hot coals. Then her stomach flipped as the cart raced towards an enormous pair of doors emblazoned with a giant K.

Just as Gabrielle braced for the crash, they swung open and swallowed her up.

# CHAPTER SEVENTEEN

The cart crashed to a stop at the end of a short dingy passage, propelling Gabrielle through the air. Her cry was cut short as she landed in a soft mound of slimy moss.

Or was it moss? For it smelled like coffee grounds and old, rotten food.

"Urgh!" As Gabrielle tried to stand, she fell face first into the muck. Something cold and smooth encircled her neck and yanked her up. A gruff little troll clutching a shepherd's crook stood before her. It yanked Gabrielle to her feet and steadied her. "Don't move!" it said, "or the muckgubbins will swallow yeh whole!"

A pair of narrow silvery eyes peered from the pile of moss. "It's alive?" Gabrielle said, with a shiver.

"Terrible things, muckgubbins. Bear that in mind if you get any sorcerous ideas. I've heard about yer witchery. Now follow me, and no dawdling!"

"I can't walk with my ankles tied together, can I?" Gabrielle hoped the troll would release her feet so she could deliver a good hard kick to its rump before fleeing.

"I'm not half as daft as I look." The troll pulled Gabrielle along by the shepherd's crook, leading her down a long black corridor lit with flaming torches. Coal dust glistened upon the walls and warm air wafted in from vents in the floor. Gabrielle's heart sank as they approached a heavy golden door, which looked both imperious and utterly sinister.

"Don't speak until he speaks to you. Got it?" The troll unhooked the crook from her neck.

"Don't speak to who?"

"The Winter King. Who else?" The troll knocked upon the door and stood back with a perturbed look.

"Enter," a voice called. It was soft as velvet but its low, silken timbre immediately struck terror into Gabrielle's heart.

The troll swallowed, opened the door, and nodded for Gabrielle to go inside. She hopped forward, stumbling as the troll shoved her in the back and slammed the door behind her.

The chamber was hollow and vast with an immense throne set before a crackling fireplace. Each step she took echoed along the jagged black rock walls that stretched up toward the distant ceiling. Gabrielle's heart skipped at the sight of two eyes glowing in the wall. A rattle of chains rang out across the room and a figure emerged from the rock and stepped into the warm glow of the fire.

He towered over her, at least eight feet tall, and he was covered with thick black fur. The horns springing from his head were broad, curled and ancient, his eyes large and narrow. They glowed fiery yellow and were flecked with orange around the black pupil that fizzled at their center. He licked the back of his fangs with a long, forked tongue. "I've got something stuck in my teeth. A pip perhaps. Or flesh, or sinew. It's been plaguing me for days."

Gabrielle felt hypnotized by his low voice. She wasn't sure if he reminded her of a goat, or a wolf. Perhaps something in between.

His cloven hooves clattered upon the cavern floor and the broken rusted chains he wore over his shoulders rattled as he approached. He sniffed deeply and gave a most wolfish smile. "It really is you!" he purred as the fire crackled and popped. His tongue lashed the air and snagged a glowing ember. He swallowed it down. "It was going to fall on your pretty little head," he said. "I cannot abide seeing my guests with their hair ablaze, it's most distressing." He bowed and rubbed his hands together, causing tiny wisps of smoke to rise from his palms. "I'm Krampus," he said. "And you are Gabrielle Greene, I've been so anxious to meet you. Now, let's get to the heart of the matter, for I have the grandest of plans for you!"

# CHAPTER EIGHTEEN

"Warm yourself by the fire," Krampus offered. Gabrielle was already warm enough but she walked toward the fireplace because it seemed best not to argue. Something tickled the nape of her neck. She spun round. Krampus loomed over her, his eyes filled with hunger, his claws outstretched, his tail thrashing like a menacing, feral cat. "Apologies. It's in my nature to stalk and creep. Especially around your kind. I'm sure you understand."

"I do," Gabrielle gazed into the fire, determined not to give into her terror. But as she heard the clatter of hooves, she twisted round to find his teeth inches from the back of her neck.

"Argh!" Krampus leaped away from Gabrielle and seized a bundle of birch twigs from the armrest of his throne. "Must... stop...trying to eat humans!" Gabrielle winced as he whipped the twigs against his back. Finally, he stopped. "That's better." He clutched the sticks tight before laying them on the floor, then he reached into the air and a tarnished old key appeared in his clawed fist. "You may remove the shackles. Your powers won't work in this room. It's proofed against witchery."

Gabrielle had no idea why he believed she had powers, but she kept her silence and unlocked the manacles, rubbing her ankles as they clattered to the floor.

"So," Krampus slumped upon his throne and crossed his hairy legs. "How did you do it?"

"How did I do what?"

"My spies in the city told me you were the worst child ever. That your list of crimes is longer than the longest of tapeworms. Which is far longer than most would care to know about. I tried to bring you here on Krampusnight, but I couldn't get you. I could see you through a sliver in your musty old curtains. I could smell you, I could hear you, and yet I couldn't find any wickedness around you at all. Usually it hangs about dastardly children like a putrid green veil, but there was nothing around you, sorceress. That's why I sent Madam Grystle, for she knows all about magical things. But you foiled her as well. How? What manner of witchcraft are you using?"

Gabrielle almost answered, he seemed so reasonable. Personable almost. But then she remembered the children toiling in the caves and she noticed the hard edge at the corner of his civil smile. "I'm not going to tell you anything until you let my brother go."

Krampus laughed, the sound warm and silken but utterly without mirth. He ground his teeth and drummed his fingers upon the side of his throne. "We caught your brother by hook and by crook. He's a thief. Therefore he must be punished."

"Percival wouldn't steal." Gabrielle folded her arms. "You're lying."

"I assure you I am not lying. It took a great deal of effort from Madam Grystle to coax that saintly little lump into committing his crime. True, she may have used smoke and mirrors, but commit a crime he did. Which is why he now finds himself in my kingdom. As do you. We knew you'd come."

Gabrielle stood tall and gazed steadily into his wicked fiery eyes. "So you cheated. Right. Well I need to get home. I've got stuff to do. Let my brother go you cheater and we'll put this all behind us and be on our way."

"You've nothing to bargain with, little girl."

"I know sorcery."

Krampus shook his head. "I don't care what magic you have at your disposal. I nabbed your brother, fair and square and that's all I need. And unless you do exactly what I tell you, I'll keep him right here scrubbing drains and hunting fleas. And there's always the trolls' toilets...they're in need of constant attention. I doubt anyone could imagine a more dank and revolting place."

"You can't keep Percival here."

"Can't I? Why ever not?" Krampus gave Gabrielle a crooked grin. "I can do whatever I like. I'm the Winter King. I can keep him here for a year, if I like."

"Well, the police are going to come looking for us. You can't just kidnap children, you know."

Krampus's laugh was loud and hearty, it echoed across the chamber, bringing down a landslide of coal dust. "Police? Your police don't police me. In case you haven't realized, you're not in *your world* of rules. You're in mine."

"They *will* come looking for us! You can't keep someone locked away for a year and expect that no one will notice."

"A year here is mere moments where you're from, girl.

Should I choose, I could keep your brother here for a dozen years and no one in your world would miss him. Is that what you want for soft plump Percival? Two score years of hard labor?"

"He's not plump."

"His soul is." Krampus's tongue flickered from his mouth and lashed another ember from the air. "But it won't be by the time we've finished with him."

Gabrielle unfolded her arms. "How do I get you to free him then?"

Krampus joined her by the fire and warmed his hands before the flames. "If you want your brother back, you'll have to do me a favor."

"What?"

"I need your sorcery and your sharp little mind to get back something that I was cheated out of. A key, stuck in the grasp of a most odious being. You probably know him as Father Christmas. That fat cunning thieving toad-"

"He's real?"

"As real as gangrene. As real as gout." Krampus's grin faltered. "He hides himself away like the thief he is. Plump and snug in Christmasland."

"Why can't you get the key back yourself?"

"I cannot go there, but you can. And you will. You want your brother back, girl? Go to Christmasland and steal back what was stolen from me."

# CHAPTER NINETEEN

"What? You want me to steal?" Gabrielle asked.

"A key. Nothing more, nothing less." Krampus smiled.

"What's it for?"

"This and that."

"And Father Christmas...took it?"

"No. He stole it, and betrayed our friendship. We were allies once, you know." A bittersweet smile played across Krampus's lips as he gazed into the fire. "We'd set out together on dark winter nights, he'd make lists of children to reward, I'd take the wicked ones and show them the errors of their ways. It worked well, until..."

"What?"

Krampus shook his head. "Nothing that concerns you. All you need to know is that I've been wronged, and you're going to be my agent of retribution. Gabrielle Greene, the wickedest child that ever was."

Gabrielle swallowed. "How will I find the key?"

"He'll keep it close. Probably in his palace. He might even wear it below that accursed beard. You can set fire to it for all I care. Just get my key."

"How will I know what it looks like?"

Krampus traced a pattern with his claw in the empty space before him. The air blistered with smoke and a molten red line formed the shape of a key. Its bow was thick and round, its shoulder stubby, seven jagged cuts ran along the bit ending in a pointed spike. "Get it for me and I'll release your brother." Krampus held his hand out. "Deal?"

"Let Percival go now and I'll do it."

It seemed for a moment that he was going to agree but a dark look crossed his face. "I won't be fooled again. Bring me the key, and our deal will be done."

"What if I get caught?"

"You won't. Not with your wits and prowess. And even if you did, you'd face no punishment. You're a child wandering in Christmasland don't forget. Just as all good children do from time to time."

"I'm not a child."

"Then what are you?"

Gabrielle had no answer, and suddenly she realized she'd lost her place. She was not a child, not like Percy, so where did that leave her exactly?

"Ah ha, I got you there, didn't I! Follow me," Krampus called out as he strode to an arched door in the corner, "to my grotto of delights and wonders. Which, though I do say so myself, puts the fat fool's stale old workshop to shame." Krampus led Gabrielle down a long winding stone tunnel. Orange light glowed from glittering glass portholes that overlooked distant streams of molten lava. They passed alcoves and niches but not a single doorway.

"Here we are." Krampus reached toward the wall and knocked three times. A hidden panel slid open onto a huge cavern. Flickering lights hung from the ceiling and a thin eerie mist hovered over the floor. "This way." Krampus led Gabrielle down a wide aisle that ran between long laboratory tables covered with test tubes, beakers, flasks and bubblers. They were filled with vivid colorful liquids, and warm welcoming fragrances wafted into the air. Gabrielle could smell honey, chestnut, rose, dust and lemon. Among the beakers in the first work station there were three long birch sticks. "They're coming along well." Krampus lifted one and brought it swishing down upon the edge of the counter. "Almost unbreakable, perfect for the relentless thrashing of the wicked and the evil."

At the next station a deck of cards lay perfectly fanned out. There seemed to be nothing particularly out of the ordinary about them, until Gabrielle picked one up. The Joker grinned and leered, then he ran his hand over his face, and transformed into a man with blonde curled hair and a mustache. He now wore finery rather than fool's clothes and the suit flickered and switched to the Jack of Spades.

"Clever eh." Pride filled Krampus's voice. "Another one of my brilliant ideas coaxed into reality by this magical lab. Those cards have saved my hide time and time again! And no matter how many times I play them, they always transform into exactly what I need to win. Have one if you like. Take it as a souvenir...or a reminder...I always win. Every single time."

Krampus escorted Gabrielle to a brazier of glowing coals. He took a deep sniff of the musty, earthy scent. "this is a coal we've been developing that burns twice as long as any other. It's both a wholesome meal, and a way of keeping my insides toasty warm on long winter nights."

A troll sat upon a tall stool at the next station. He pulled a length of licorice from a bowl and chewed upon it, before checking his tongue in a small round mirror. It was streaked inky blue.

"We need to find a way of stopping the perilous blue streak syndrome. Then I can market my selection of sweet treats to a wider audience," Krampus explained. "Feel free to help yourself." He walked on. "And then we'll visit an old friend who's working on a way to keep me safe from the prying eyes your people fill their world with."

"Eyes?" Gabrielle asked.

"Yes, the ghastly mechanical things that are always watching and cataloging everything."

"Do you mean cameras?"

"Indeed. I simply cannot allow them to capture me, I'm not meant to be seen. Except by those due for punishment." He stopped before a troll in a long white smock. It glanced up from a leather bound journal and gave Krampus a salute. "I'm honored you've chosen to visit my liege, my-"

"Enough." Krampus held up a hand. "Fizzlenee, meet Gabrielle Greene, the girl who eluded me. Until now."

Fizzlenee's eyes lit up. "How did you evade the master? What spells did you use, did-"

"There's no time for questions," Krampus said. "Gabrielle needs to sneak over the wall, and into the fat one's lair. She must be as stealthy as a fox. Can you give her the means to do this?"

"Indeed, master!"

Gabrielle yelped as Fizzlenee pulled a hair from her head.

"I could give her a disguise," Fizzlenee said. "Make her look like an elf, perhaps."

"That should work." Krampus jumped onto a desk. It buckled beneath him as he leaned over a flask of bubbling mauve water and stuck his finger in. He flinched as glittering sparks rose into the air. "Ouch!" Krampus tucked his finger under his armpit.

"Ohhh no! There's all sorts of goodness about, my lord, it would be best not to touch anything" Fizzlenee said as he leaned over and sniffed Gabrielle's forehead. "Yes, we can work with you."

Krampus led Gabrielle to the far end of the room, it looked like the clothing section of a department store. Black capes, waistcoats and leggings hung upon hangers and rack. Hats were carefully displayed on stands, most of which had holes punched into the sides, to accommodate Krampus's great arching horns.

Cutty!" Krampus cried. "Cutty!"

Another troll appeared, she was female and haughty looking. She gazed at Gabrielle through half moon glasses and produced a tape measure from her pocket. "And what am I creating for this...human?"

"Give her the garb of an elf," Fizzlenee called from his bench, "I'll make her a beard. Then all I'll need to do is make a few alterations to her face and slice-"

"Hold on." Gabrielle stepped back. "You're turning me into an elf? With a beard?"

"Indeed." Fizzlenee nodded sharply.

"Why?" Gabrielle asked.

"So you'll blend in, of course," Cutty replied.

"But you don't make him blend into our world,' Gabrielle nodded to Krampus. "You just make sure no one sees him. Can't you do that for me too?" The thought of that beard was making her chin itch.

"I suppose so," Fizzlenee conceded. "But you're a human, how can we make sure no one sees you?"

"Well, if my mission is to be a thief, then you might as

well make me into a cat burglar." Gabrielle imagined a sleek outfit to blend with the night. "Or a ninja. A cat burgling ninja! I'll need gloves for scaling walls. And an all-in-one outfit that keeps me warm and lets me move quickly and silently. And it should all be in black."

"You see." Krampus wolfish grin widened. "Such imagination and ambition!"

"Quite, and wit." Cutty said, as she peered down her nose at Gabrielle. "Black will stand out against the snow,"

"True," Gabrielle agreed.

"Then make her a hooded coat and boots, all in white." Krampus hopped down from the bench and stood before Gabrielle. "You'll make the most perfect plunderer. Gabrielle Greene; the thief of Christmas!"

Cutty removed a length of ebony cloth from a tall cupboard and took it over to a worktable. After she smoothed it out flat, she picked up a huge pair of scissors. The scraps fell to the floor and her fingers were a whirring blur as the scissors snipped out the pieces she needed. Next she took a thread and needle and sewed, the motion so fast it made Gabrielle feel dizzy. When she was finished, Cutty held up a sleek black all-in-one outfit that glimmered in the air. She laid it upon the worktable and took a long piece of white cloth from the cupboard and carried it to a large cast iron sewing machine, and began to sew. Within minutes she stood and laid a beautiful white hooded coat next to the clothes. Then she gathered lengths of fur and fashioned a pair of boots for Gabrielle.

Fizzlenee filled a small glass with liquids from several of the beakers. The potion bubbled as it turned purple, then red, then green. He placed his thumb over the end and shook it, before sprinkling a few glimmering drops upon the coat. It shone and twinkled, as if it had been fashioned from a drift of shimmering snow.

Cutty gestured for Gabrielle to take her new clothes and she led her to a dressing room. "Put them on," she said.

They fitted perfectly. Gabrielle wrapped the coat around herself and imagined creeping stealthily through the wintery landscape. Krampus clapped as Gabrielle emerged from the dressing room. "Perfect! Now, follow me. It's time for you to make your journey."

# CHAPTER TWENTY

Krampus led Gabrielle through a door and down a long a tunnel. They stopped before a large window set into the rock wall. On the other side she could see the giant sink and a group of children scrubbing and cleaning the seemingly endless number of dishes piled up like a ceramic mountain.

A small sorrowful boy stood at the end of the line, drying an enormous plate with a tea towel the size of a blanket.

"Percival!" Gabrielle reached out to rap her knuckles upon the window but Krampus seized her hand. "No," he said. "Not until you bring me the key. Remember your objective, for you only have one and it's of the utmost importance."

Gabrielle glanced back to her brother. *Be strong Perce. I'll get you out of here.* Percival began to turn her way, as if he sensed she was there but Krampus scooted her past the window. "This way." He led Gabrielle up a sharply sloped corridor that was sealed off by a rock wall with a small red tin panel to one side. Krampus placed his hand upon the panel and a hidden door slid open. "Another of my troll's inventions," he beamed. "Sometimes I just stand here opening and closing the door, just for the sheer fun of it."

"That sounds exciting." After seeing Percival, so small and miserable, Gabrielle was having trouble disguising her sarcasm and anger.

They entered a large round cavern that reminded Gabrielle of an aircraft hangar, only the space was filled with dozens of sleighs and sleds rather than planes. Each one was painted jet black, swathed in jagged spikes and utterly dwarfed by the monstrous sleigh that filled the center of the cavern.

It was colossal; the brush bow swept up and back into an elaborate curl with long cast iron prongs that made it look like an otherworldly beast. The runners were sleek and polished with scrolling bramble like rungs and a great fur lined seat rose up in the center like a throne.

Krampus climbed aboard and gestured for Gabrielle to sit upon the pile of furs at the front. "Hold on," he barked, as he pulled a lever at the side of his throne.

The grinding din of machinery and clockwork filled the air and the ground shook as a platform rose, taking them up through the mountain. A deep rumble rang out, then the rock walls and ceiling juddered as they began to slide open. The brightness of the wintry blue sky stung Gabrielle's eyes and she shivered as the frosty air swirled around her.

The platform thunked to a stop and she looked out over the top of the mountain. A shadow fell over her, cast by the great arching granite horns modeled perfectly after the mighty Krampus.

A howling chorus filled the air. Gabrielle thought it was the roaring wind, until she realized it was coming from a row of wooden lodges. Krampus pulled a bone-white horn from the furs at his feet. As he blew, a deep, resonant trumpeting burst forth. It made Gabrielle think of an angry elephant as it echoed across the mountain top. "Bring my wolves," Krampus shouted. "Hurry!" He placed a pair of goggles over his eyes, and then, with a deft sleight of hand, he produced a pair for Gabrielle. "Put these on."

The doors of a nearby lodge burst opened and a team of trolls emerged, leading six keen black wolves on thick taut hide leashes. They harnessed the writhing beasts to the sleigh. The wolves panted and lunged as the troll handed the reins to Krampus.

"Hang on" Krampus called. It took Gabrielle a moment to realize he was talking to her but she did as she was told as he cried out, "Hike! Mush!"

The wolves ears pricked up and they fell into formation, bowing their heads as they pulled the sleigh along behind them.

Soon they were scurrying through the snow and the dry powdery flakes flew up behind them like a wake of white confetti. The high arching bow kept most of the snow from getting into Gabrielle's eyes, and the goggles stopped the rest. But it didn't take long for her face to become frosty and numb in the chilly air.

They hurtled down the slope, the land rushing by in a dizzying blur. Gabrielle's scream was snatched away by the wind as it screeched in her ears.

The wolves lurched down the hill, the crunch of the churning snow almost deafening. "Faster!" Krampus called as he cracked the reins and the wolves sped across the vast icy expanse. "Mush!" Krampus growled. "Hike!"

The sleigh rattled and rumbled and trees whipped by as they shot through a forest. Their branches were merrily laden with snow but the spaces between them were dark and sinister. Every now and then Gabrielle caught sight of flickering eyes, and figures trudging through the snow. She shivered with fear, until she remembered who was sitting behind her. *Krampus, the King of Winter.* Surely there couldn't be anything more feared than him in this strange, dark world.

The forest began to thin out, the trees grew smaller and their lush and green needles filled the air with the vibrant scent of pine. Stars, baubles and tinsel hung from the branches and glimmered in the afternoon sun. Krampus barked and bellowed but his words were lost to the baying howls of the wolves. His face wrinkled with disgust and he held his nose.

"What?" Gabrielle asked. She could smell nothing but pine and crisp fresh air.

Krampus nodded his head toward a giant tree towering up upon the crest of the hill.

The wolves slowed and brought the sleigh sliding to a halt. Krampus released the reins and the wolves laid down in the snow. Steam poured from their slathering mouths as he called to them "Rest, my beasts, for soon we'll-" He clamped a hand over his mouth and retched.

"What's wrong?" Gabrielle asked, both mystified and alarmed.

He held a hand up and shook his head, his nostrils flaring. A soft warm breeze wafted over the hill bringing a rich sweet scent and a sound of distant chiming bells. "Urgh,"Krampus tore off his goggles and wiped his watering eyes. He looked as if he were about to say something, but doubled over in his chair. "Can't...stand...the...stench of Christmas!"

Gabrielle sniffed the air. It really *did* smell like Christmas. She sighed as she caught the spicy notes of cinnamon, tangy mandarin oranges, fragrant woodsmoke, zesty pine, crisp peppermint, and juicy roast turkey.

The rolling hills peaked and fell among a fall of fat lazy snow flakes and she could see a distant forest of fir trees. Nestled beyond them was a majestic glacial white structure adorned with parapets and elegant spindly towers. "Is that where Father Christmas lives?"

"Yes, that's where you'll find the lowdown traitorous dog." Krampus grumbled as he spat blue-black bile into the snow. "I can't stand this stench any longer. Scale the wall. Find the city. Get the key. Yes?"

"What wall?"

Krampus jumped down, gathered a handful of snow and packed it into a ball and threw it over the hill. The snowball seemed to strike the very air itself, then a towering stone wall appeared. It stretched on for as far as Gabrielle could see, before it glimmered and vanished again.

"You'll have to climb it," Krampus said.

"It's incredibly high."

"So?" Krampus demanded. "You're a sneak thief, aren't you? You have powers, don't you?" He narrowed his eyes.

"I'll do it," Gabrielle said. "I'll get the key, and you've promised to let Percival go. In one piece."

"That's the deal. And unlike some I could mention, I keep my word." Krampus retched again and screwed up his face in revulsion as silvery tears fell from his eyes. "Go," he said. "Christmas Eve will be here before we know it, and I need my key back before it dawns." He clapped his hands and the wolves padded over. He seized the reins, climbed up to his throne, reached into the furs at his feet and threw a black egg to Gabrielle. She caught it. It was sort of like a goose egg but it was hard, pitted and warm to the touch, even through her glove. "What's this?"

"I'd have thought a sorceress of your stature would know exactly what that is." Krampus eyed Gabrielle suspiciously. "Crack it open as soon as you have my key."

"Ah," Gabrielle said. "It's one of *those.*" She nodded and slipped the egg into her pocket and started down the hill.

"Find the key and be quick about it, girl," Krampus called. "Because if you don't, your brother will find himself dredging the drain of eternal slime and unspeakable ooze. And I may decide to send you there to join him." He cracked his reins. The wolves lunged, taking his sleigh down the hill. With a frosty gust of the wind he was gone, leaving Gabrielle alone in the shadow of a giant tree.

# CHAPTER TWENTY-ONE

The snowy land stretched before Gabrielle like a sheet of paper rolling out toward a glimmering forest. The trees were festooned with colored lights that danced and twinkled below the grey sky. It was beautiful and enchanting. Gabrielle wished Percival was here to see it, instead of being locked below that desolate mountain, scrubbing dishes or whatever other hideous chore he'd been given.

She descended the hill, scooped up a snowball and threw it. It struck the air before her, and the towering wall appeared. Gabrielle walked toward it slowly and placed her hands upon the surface. The palms of her gloves stuck to the wall as if they were made from velcro. She climbed, placing one hand over the other. As she reached the top, she pulled herself up and balanced upon her haunches.

The wind blew softly, bringing a waft of nutmeg, chocolate, and holly. Gabrielle scaled down the other side of the wall and dropped the last few feet, landing as gracefully as a cat. She pulled her hood up to keep herself hidden and made her way through the billowy drifts of snow. Her boots and leggings kept her surprisingly warm and her long coat made for ideal camouflage.

Gabrielle was halfway up the slope and about to enter the forest, when she saw the figures. There were five, each round and white with dark staring eyes.

*How can they see me?* Gabrielle glanced around and winced when she saw her tracks in the snow.

The figures continued to gaze at her. Two of them were taller than Gabrielle, the other three much smaller. Then she spotted their bright orange noses and realized they were a family of snowmen. The snow woman had long flowing white hair, the snow boys wore peaked hats while and the snow girl beside them had icy braids tied with bows. Their pebble eyes were as round as the buttons upon their winter coats as they gaped at Gabrielle. The snow man tipped his black bowler hat as they turned and shuffled away. Gabrielle stood and watched them, entranced until she remembered why she was here. To hide and steal. A sneak thief in an enchanted land. She waited for them to vanish into the trees, before trudging away in the opposite direction.

This forest was completely different to the dark wooded maze where she'd encountered the Christmas Cat for it looked like an illustration from a merry winter fairy tale. The trees were tall and bushy and red and gold lanterns ornamented the topmost branches, throwing soft diffused light across the snowy ground. Holly and brightly colored baubles adorned each bough and tiny silver bells chimed in soft, intricate melodies. Tawny-brown reindeer flitted through the trees. Gabrielle craned her neck trying to catch a glimpse of their noses, hoping to find them glowing red, but alas they were dull and black.

A flurry of snow fluttered down like cherry blossoms as Gabrielle approached a clearing filled with tall pointed buildings. They were shaped like pixie hats and painted bright red and green. Warm yellow light spilled through latticed windows and tiny figures meandered through the village.

"Elves?" Gabrielle whispered. What else could they be? They were about the same height as the trolls but leaner, and something in their expressions put her in mind of children. Sullen, downcast children with long sour scowls.

She tip-toed through the snow and made her way along the outskirts of the village, noting that the paint on the walls was not quite as bright as she'd first thought. Indeed it was cracked and faded. The doors were buckled and warped, the windows pitted and filthy. The place was like a dilapidated seaside resort, once glorious but now well past its prime.

With a ruckus, three elves in long green coats stumbled out of a low squat building near the square. The sign read: "The Jingling Bell" and a flyer in the window advertised:

*Happy Hour; Butterscotch a penny a pint!*

Their faces were bleary, red, and melancholy. One stumbled into another and within moments the pair were rolling through the snow in a blur of fists. A stout stern-looking elf leapt from the doorway of The Jingling Bell and forced them apart. "If yeh going to fight, do it away from my establishment!"

The two elves staggered off in opposite directions, then one stooped down and gathered up a snow ball. He let it fly and it hit the other in the back of the head with a hard, solid thump.

The stricken elf fell face down. It lay still for a moment, then staggered up and grabbed handfuls of snow. The elf compacted it into the largest snow ball Gabrielle had ever seen before throwing it wildly. The snowball shot past Gabrielle's head and reached its target smack bang in the middle of his face. The elf gave a muffled howl through its snow-filled mouth before lurching toward the other.

"It's probably time to leave," Gabrielle whispered, and tip-toed back among the trees. The magical wonder she'd felt died away. Somehow the sight of the elven village left her with an even bleaker feeling than Krampus's dark wild lands. Where were the rosy cheeked elves who made presents and laughed? The jolly magical beings filled with Christmas cheer throughout the year?

The forest grew dense, slowing Gabrielle's progress. She hopped over fallen logs that lay in her path, like giant swiss rolls covered in icing. She tromped through dells and banks of snow until she came across a smooth icy path. Sled and horse tracks had compacted snow and a tall wooden sign jutted out of a snow bank. The arrows pointed in opposite directions. One read *The City of Christmas*, and the other *The Scary Dark Borders of Krampus.*

Gabrielle headed towards the city of Christmas and picked up her pace as the sky began to grow dark. She wondered if it was night back in the world she'd left. Then she thought of her uncle, and her parents. This was all their fault. They should be the ones rescuing Percival from this dire place, not her. None of it would have happened if it wasn't for them. "Percival would be safe," Gabrielle muttered, "and I wouldn't be here all on my own. I can't do everything. I can't-" She stopped as the weight of it all sank down upon her shoulders. Tears pricked her eyes as she thought of Percival and the other children trapped below the dark mountain. It wasn't fair. None of it was fair.

She looked up as something flitted upon the tree before her. A robin. It hopped along the branch, cocked its head and regarded her with shiny black eyes. Gabrielle wiped her tears away with the back of her glove, and carried on. "I'll get this sorted Perce, and then we'll go home."

The trees that grew along the path were tall, their knobbly brown trunks towering up and the tops of their branches bubblegum pink in the growing dusk. Sap oozed from the bark in amber knots; somehow Gabrielle found the pine scent reassuring. She broke off a piece and was about to hold it up to the light, when a bloodcurdling scream rang across the forest.

Gabrielle's heart raced as another cry echoed through the trees only to be swallowed by the dying light.

# CHAPTER TWENTY-TWO

Muffled words punctuated the screams and it was hard to make them out, apart from one word. "*Help!*"

Gabrielle leapt from the path and trudged through the snow toward the ruckus.

Down in the dell below, resting at the base of a tree, was the biggest snowball she'd ever seen. She followed the trail from where it has rolled, picking up more and more snow until it had finally come to a stop.

Gabrielle could see a striped pair of leggings and a tiny pair of wiggling clogs poking out of the screaming snowball. "I'm on my way!" she shouted as she slid down the hill.

"I can't see. Just the light. Nothing but the light." The voice was shrill, ragged and distinctly female. "Is this the end? Am I dead? I'm not ready to go. Please, I'm not ready!"

Gabrielle reached into the snowball and tore it apart. She jumped as a hand reached through and grabbed her glove. A pair of bright green eyes peered from a ruddy, upside-down face. "Are you an angel?" The elf asked as the snowball tumbled away. She fell with a squeal and lay sprawled out in the snow.

"Here." Gabrielle clasped the elf's hand and pulled her to her feet.

The elf scrubbed the snow from her coat, and shot Gabrielle a bewildered look. "Are you the Christmas spirit?" the elf asked. And then her face fell. "Or a witch from beyond the wall?"

"I'm Gabrielle. Gabrielle Greene."

"Are you?" The elf looked doubtful. "And how did you manage to get into Christmasland? There haven't been humans here since...since before everything went wrong."

"I climbed the wall."

"That's impossible. The wall cannot be breached. Or so he said, but then his word isn't worth toffee anymore. Did you use sorcery?"

"I used my gloves." Gabrielle held them up and allowed the elf to inspect them.

"They look handy, if you'll pardon the pun. Where did you get them from?"

"My...my uncle gave them to me."

The elf gave her a suspicious look as she brushed the remaining snow from her clothes. "So where are you going, Gabrielle Greene? If that really is your name."

"I'm going to Christmas. Is it far?"

"It's close. That's where I was going before I took my tumble. It was the anger, you see. It overwhelmed me. I know I shouldn't have, but I kicked a tree and then I lost my footing."

"Why were you angry?"

The elf gave Gabrielle a withering look that suggested Gabrielle should know exactly why she was so angry. "Maybe it had something to do with all of us being sacked and replaced by that damnable device. Which according to him is exactly what we all want. To sit around all day doing nothing but drinking cheap butterscotch. Well some might enjoy that, but I don't and neither does anyone else I know. We loved our jobs, and now they're gone, and everything's fallen apart."

"I don't understand. Who sacked you?"

"The man in the red tunic. Mr. Haughty Christmas."

"Father Christmas?"

"That's the one," the elf growled.

"Why did he sack you?"

"How would I know? He hasn't deigned to talk to us for a very long time. And why would he? We're just the little people who wrap presents and tie pretty bows. What do we matter?" A bright gleam lit her eyes, "But we do matter. And I'm going to tell him that. So if you want to get to the city, follow me, Gabrielle Greene. If that's who you really are." The elf began to climb the forested slope.

Gabrielle followed and soon they reached the path. The elf stormed ahead, the tips of her ears bright red against the glittering snow. "Hurry!" she called. Gabrielle caught her up and the elf continued to seethe with anger and indignation as she stomped along.

. . .

They emerged from the forest to an expanse of thick white snow and beyond it a huge wall that encircled a city of tall round buildings. At the center stood a palace, its walls the color of vanilla ice cream with towers and spires that soared up into the evening sky. Red and green banners hung down and golden light blazed from hundreds of elegant arched windows. "Is that where Father Christmas lives?" Gabrielle asked.

"Yes. That's the palace where he lords it over the land of Christmas."

"Is the whole land called Christmas?" Gabrielle asked.

"That's been its name these last few centuries, but it's had many other names. Most of which I can't recall."

They trudged through the snow to a huge arched gateway, and entered the city. The cobbled streets were dusted with frost and everything was perfectly silent. Street lamps lined the winding streets, but not a single light shone in any of the buildings, except the palace. Occasionally, Gabrielle caught sight of figures flitting from doorways or gazing from windows, but the city was mostly deserted. The paint on the buildings was peeling, and the tiny wooden doors were as warped as the ones in the elven village.

"Everything's gone to chaos," the elf said. "Everything save for the palace. His halls are swept so clean you can see your reflection in them, and the paint on the walls is as fresh as mountain air. Yes, His Honor likes to live as a king while everything around him festers."

"Why is it so quiet?"

The elf looked as if she were about to respond when a deafening clamor tore through the air.

Gabrielle clamped her hands over her ears.

It was a mechanical sound, like great grinding gears turning inside a clanking apparatus driven by wildly spinning springs and wheels. She imagined a vast hole in the ground leading down to the center of the world and all its workings.

They jumped as a booming explosion rang out. Silence followed, save for the beating wings of chalk-white birds that swept up over the city.

"What was that?" Gabrielle lowered her hands from her ears.

"That was the end...of everything." The elf shook her head. Her anger was gone now. "I thought I could stop it, but I can't." She turned and fled down the street.

"Wait!" Gabrielle called.

But it was too late.

She was gone.

# CHAPTER
# TWENTY-THREE

There was nowhere else for Gabrielle to go but onwards. She turned a bend in the cobbled street and stood before the palace. A set of stone steps led to an enormous red door studded with copper nails. Marble statues of reindeer were mounted on both sides of the stairway, rearing up in graceful, regal poses.

Gabrielle turned the door handle. It was locked. She reached for the swan-shaped knocker, but then remembered why Krampus had sent her. To be stealthy. To steal.

She walked to the side of the building. Far above her was an arched window with the sash jutting out. It looked like the window was ajar. Gabrielle took a deep breath and placed a gloved hand upon the wall, her heart pounding as she began to climb. The wind screeched all around her like a banshee. Going higher was too risky, despite the reassuring grip of her gloves, so she paused and waited for the wind to slow, before continuing.

Up and up she climbed, until the icy cobbled street grew disturbingly distant below her.

Gabrielle reached the window and pulled it open as wide as it would go. She hoisted herself up, slipped through the opening and fell to the plush rug below.

It was a large study with a wide mahogany desk and rows of bookcases filled with red and green bound books. The room held a rich nutty scent of polish, and every surface was immaculately free of even the slightest speck of dust. It was stately but it had a snug feeling as well, with comfortable looking chairs and a coat stand that stood by the door. Upon it hung a deep red cape with white fur trim.

Was it *his?*

Gabrielle slipped from the room and made her way along a corridor but slowed as something clanked above her and a peculiar trundling sound came through the ceiling. Gabrielle stepped lightly up a short flight of stairs, the thick carpeting masking her footsteps.

The clanking grew louder as she entered an enormous chamber with emerald green walls. Flurries of snowflakes fell past a tall arched window and a fire blazed in a cozy hearth mostly obscured by a colossal wingback chair. Snowy white hair peeked over the top of the chair and a hand reached toward a small control panel set into the armrest. The chair shook and rattled upon the floor, producing the clanking sound she'd heard from downstairs.

She peered round the side. A great, portly man sat before the fire with his long frothy white beard resting on his fat round belly. Firelight glistened in the pince-nez glasses resting upon his red bulbous nose. He balanced a plate of sugar cookies upon his lap and chomped one in half, sending an avalanche of crumbs into his bushy beard.

"No you don't!" He fished the crumbs out one by one and popped them into his mouth, before setting the plate on a small side table. His great pudgy hand gripped a lever and the chair leaned back further, bringing his striped socked feet up before the fire.

He was the very picture of contentment and indulgence, and yet his eyes held a strangely melancholy and haunted look.

There was no question. This was the man whose great deeds had filled Gabrielle's dreams, starting each September as soon as the weather cooled, until the deepest frosts of December. At least until the last few years when she'd assumed he was nothing but a myth.

And here he was, picking crumbs from his beard.

He seemed bedraggled and unwell. Tired and sad. His red eyes almost matching his tunic. He glanced at the long scarlet hat hanging from a hook upon the wall, then to the golden key beside it...

"Oh!" Gabrielle's boot struck the corner of a bookcase as she edged forward.

His chair groaned as he spun round to face her.

Surprise, bewilderment and anger flashed through his eyes as he struggled to his feet. He was much taller than Gabrielle had expected, and rounder too.

"Who are you?" He boomed as he lumbered towards her, his huge shadow blocking out the light, as if a great dark cloud had passed across the world.

# CHAPTER
# TWENTY-FOUR

"Hi!" Gabrielle said. She didn't know what else to say.

Father Christmas gave her gloves, coat and boots a suspicious glance. Finally his expression softened and the cloud of darkness surrounding him rippled and faded. "My apologies," he said. "I thought you were an assassin. I've been expecting one to come calling."

"An assassin?"

"An assassin. Or a thief. Both steal. One more severely than the other." He gave Gabrielle a short-lived smile. "I can see you're no killer. Did one of the elves bring you? We haven't held any tours, not for many, many moons. Which is entirely my fault," he sighed. "Have you come to claim a gift?"

Gabrielle glanced at the key gleaming upon the wall. "I, erm-"

"Don't be awkward. I give gifts. That's what I do." He held his hand out for her to shake. "Call me Nicholas if you like. That's one of my more recent names."

"Gabrielle." She shook his hand. It was as warm and soft as dough.

"Charmed to meet you." He smiled but his eyes still held a gleam of sadness. And then he clapped his hands and grinned so hard the ends of his great mustache began to curl. "So what can I get for you?" he gazed at Gabrielle for a moment, before adding. "Ah, but I see you've already used your wish. And not so long ago."

"My wish?"

Father Christmas led Gabrielle to a pair of velvet curtains that covered the far wall. He pulled a rope and they opened to reveal a large painted map of the world. Tiny little gold and silver lights, the size of a pinprick, twinkled upon the map. "Silver represents people yet to use their wishes, gold shows those who have. You'd be a gold speck if you were still in your world, but I don't need the map to know you've spent your wish. A realized wish leaves the most particular scent. Think treacle and lemon, and how the air smells after a storm."

"I don't think I made any wishes." Gabrielle folded her arms.

"I promise you did. Still, now you're here I could probably give you another. And show off my machine whilst I do." Father Christmas motioned for Gabrielle to follow him to a pair of glass doors. He threw them open and ushered her to the narrow balcony beyond. "You see?"

A long silver structure stood below. It started at the palace and sprawled out to the distant forest like a crash-landed spaceship. Far below her feet she could see a huge metal dome covered in rivets and a conveyer belt under a long glass ceiling that stretched out toward the forest. Tiny metallic figures stood on either side of the belt. They had perfectly round heads and black button eyes, and wide smiling mouths. Each sat slumped against the conveyer belt as if sleeping.

"There," Father Christmas said, "the Christmas machine in all its glory!"

"Are those robots?"

"Well, I call them my little automated helper friends. And what helpers they are, no matter rain or shine or night or day!"

"But I thought the elves were supposed to be your helpers."

"They were, and they did a most splendid job. But now they're free to do as they please. Except for the one night of the year when I need help with deliveries. Yes, we all have it so much easier now." Father Christmas rubbed his belly absently. "We barely have to lift a finger. And that's just how I like it."

"Do you think the elves are happy?"

"Happy enough." Father Christmas ushered Gabrielle back toward the doors. "Get inside. It's cold enough to freeze a dragon's heart out here." He stepped into the room and smiled as he closed the doors behind him. "Now, we should see about your gift. That's what you came here for, wasn't it?"

Gabrielle nodded quickly, almost forgetting the real purpose of her visit.

Father Christmas paused before the book cases. Hundreds and hundreds of dark red and green tomes filled the shelves.

"Gabrielle..." Father Christmas leaned against a wheeled ladder. "Greene. Where are you?" He ran his finger along the spines, pulled down a hefty tome and leafed through the pages. "Here we are. I see you're a cat lover, although you're also partial to owls. It's a close call, but cats definitely win."

"Win what?"

"My books contain all manner of fascinating facts about people. Not just names and addresses. Favorite animals, birds, colors, or in your brother's case this year; ships in bottles. These books contain the names of every single person alive today, as well as everything they love. Naturally the entries change over time, just as people do. For instance, I see that three years ago you loved hedgehogs."

"How do you know that?"

"Magic." He winked.

"But why do you need to know which animals I like?"

"All will be revealed." Father Christmas slid the book back onto the shelf and stooped over a writing desk. He took a fountain pen and dipped it into an inkwell, and wrote something on a strip of paper. He neatly folded the paper and placed it in a cigar-shaped tin canister and fed it into a brass tube that jutted out from the wall. It vanished with a rush of air and a distant rattle. Father Christmas pulled a lever on the control panel by his seat. "Now watch!"

A grinding, clanking din came from outside. It was the same noise Gabrielle had heard when she'd entered the city.

"It shouldn't take them a tick!" Father Christmas shouted over the hubbub. He grinned and paced up and down. Moments later the din stopped and the tin canister shot out of the tube, straight into Father Christmas's outstretched hand. He unscrewed the lid and removed a box. It was wrapped in midnight blue paper decorated with a bright red bow. "Merry Christmas. Even if it is a little early."

"Thanks!" Gabrielle took the tiny box. "So you really do bring presents. I thought it was my dad."

"I don't deliver *all your* presents." Father Christmas held up a single finger. "Just one. Open it."

Gabrielle pulled the ribbon and carefully unwrapped the paper to reveal a gold foiled package about the size of a match box. She slid it open. Inside a small teak cat lay upon a bed of soft white cotton wool. Gabrielle held it up to the light, and for the briefest moment it winked at her. And then it became a still, solid figurine once more. "She's lovely. Thank you!"

"Keep it safe."

"I will," Gabrielle promised.

"Not the figurine, it's merely a vessel. The type of trinket people find on Christmas Day and forget about as their eyes seek larger, shinier prizes. But that's okay. All that matters is that they open the gift, for then the true gift is given."

"What's the *true* gift?"

"A wish." He tapped his chest. "It ends up in here. Deep inside your heart if you have space for it. And there it waits, until you use it. If you use it. For so many of your kind have forgotten how to wish and dream. And then there's those who fritter their dreams on needless things, *I wish it would stop raining, I wish I was thinner, I wish it was Friday.*"

"I don't remember making any wishes like that." Gabrielle would certainly have remembered if she had.

"Really?" Father Christmas folded his arms. "You don't remember making a wish just a few nights ago? A wish to be somewhere else, somewhere far away? And didn't you receive that wish?"

Gabrielle swallowed as she remembered the night when those boys tried to steal Percival's bag.

"I see you remember."

"I didn't know it would actually work!" Gabrielle felt cheated.

"I've never understood the point in making wishes if you don't believe they'll come true? Anyway, it doesn't matter, because now you have a second chance. But it must be spent before Christmas Day, because that's when the new wishes are gifted, and you can only have one at a time. So choose swiftly but be careful what you wish for." He pulled a pocket watch from his tunic. "Ah, it's chocolate o'clock. Would you care to join me?"

"Sure." Gabrielle grinned until her eyes drifted toward the key upon the wall and she remembered why she was here. She jumped as Father Christmas clapped his hands.

"Stark!" He boomed.

A tiny, stooped elf trudged into the room. He had a long pointed face crowned by corkscrews of coppery hair, and a pair of bright blue eyes. The elf bowed, grabbing his hat as it slid from his head. He righted it and glanced up at Father Christmas. "Master?"

"This young lady is Gabrielle Greene, she's my guest and we'd both quite like a nice mug of hot chocolate. And perhaps a plate of pies while we're at it."

"*More* pies, master?" The elf's voice held a dry, pointed tone as his eyes flitted over Father Christmas's bulging stomach.

"Why ever not?" Father Christmas's cheeks colored. "Sweets are one of the only comforts I have these days." He sighed, as he watched Stark leave the room. "And what dark days they are. Darker than the deepest cave in the midst of winter."

"Why?"

"Because of regretful things and poor decisions. A friend who became a foe and turned into an enemy. Every night I expect to find a flashing blade at my throat, or to wake with a pillow over my face."

"Why would anyone want to do that?"

The last trace of jollity left Father Christmas's gaze. "I don't want to talk about it."

Gabrielle glanced at the key and looked away. "I..." She stuttered, not knowing quite what to say as Stark returned with the hot chocolate.

Father Christmas shook his head. "My taste for something sweet has passed," he nodded to Gabrielle. "But you should have your drink. Mine too if you so desire. And then you must be on your way. Take a keepsake from the palace if you like, for everything must go." He gave Gabrielle a weak, half smile as he returned to his cozy fireside chair.

He put his feet up and sank back into his seat. Moments later the room echoed with the rasp and steady wheeze of his snores.

# CHAPTER TWENTY-FIVE

"Your chocolate," Stark said.

Gabrielle took the tall wide mug. It was warm, even through her gloves. "Thank you."

Stark gave a short, sharp nod and trudged from the room. The hot chocolate was sweet and the cream on top thick and soft. Gabrielle took another sip and gazed at Father Christmas, who lay slumped in his chair, his hair trailing over the back.

Then she glanced at the key as a distant clattering came from the kitchen. Gabrielle set her drink down and crept towards the wall where it hung. She almost had it unhooked when Father Christmas snuffled in his sleep. Guilt pricked her heart. He looked so tired, so...finished.

*I can't steal from him.*

And then she thought of Percival, stuck inside that nightmarish mountain.

Gabrielle shook her head. It was just an old key. It wasn't as if she were stealing his riches. He wouldn't miss it surely. She reached for it, but stopped once more.

What was it for, and why was it so valuable to Krampus? Gabrielle thought about waking Father Christmas. Perhaps if she explained what was going on, he'd be able to help, and then she wouldn't have to steal anything. But how could a man who was so washed up and defeated help her? No, clearly all he wanted to do was sit back in his chair gorging on pastries, king of his crumbling city.

Gabrielle snatched the key from its hook and stole from the room. It was light in her fingers. Unlike her heart, which had never felt heavier.

. . .

Father Christmas opened a single eye and watched Gabrielle as she slipped out the door, leaving nothing but the faint scent of coal that had clung to her strange white coat.

As he heard her bound off the last step of the staircase, he sat up. The hook where his key had hung for so many years was now empty.

With resignation he gazed into the dying fire. "So be it," he said, as the light outside faded, as if some great beast had engulfed the world and swallowed the palace whole. He sighed. "Everything must go."

# CHAPTER
# TWENTY-SIX

Gabrielle rushed down the stairs toward a wide hall with a gleaming white marble floor. The ruby-red walls were covered in sparkling, twinkling stars and festooned with glossy boughs of holly. She crossed the room heading for the great studded door at the far side. Gabrielle pulled the great brass handle, slipped through and closed it softly behind her.

The snowy ground seemed blue and almost luminescent below the darkening sky. She found the trail of footprints she'd left earlier and wondered what would have happened if she'd chosen another path; one of openness, honesty and trust. Guilt whispered and nagged in the back of her mind as she walked through the silent city and gazed back at the palace. "It's too late now." She thrust her hand into her pocket to make sure the key was still there and her fingers closed around something cold, heavy, and sharply ridged.

The egg.

Recalling Krampus's strange instructions, Gabrielle strode to the wall of a tall round house and cracked the egg upon it. She expected it to collapse into soft stringy goo, but it remained intact. Gabrielle cracked it again and a tiny fracture appeared, highlighted by a bright flickering orange-red glow. She cracked the egg again and it split in two. Gabrielle flinched as a tiny, ruffled black bird with chalky white horns blinked up at her from the shell. Its inky eyes were filled with avarice and hunger as it sniffed the air. "Key?" It hissed.

"What?"

"Key?" The bird cried, anger lacing its minuscule voice. "I take key to Krampus!"

Gabrielle reached into her pocket and pulled the key out by its long chain. "I've got it here."

The bird narrowed its bulbous eyes, and snapped at the key. Gabrielle snatched it back. "No, I'll give it to Krampus myself, thank you. Go and tell him I have it, and that I want my brother back." The bird screwed up its eyes and expelled an angry caw, followed by a puff of smoke. It stomped its tiny feet up and down, shattering the remains of the egg shell, before flapping its wings and rising unsteadily into the air. It fixed Gabrielle with a final, malevolent glare before flying off into the leaden gloom.

Gabrielle glanced back as she continued through the forlorn, empty city. The palace was dark now but for a single light flickering in Father Christmas's chambers. "I'm sorry," She whispered, and she meant it.

· · ·

Gabrielle wandered into the stable yards that lined the city's wall. Milk-white stallions peered from the stalls, their breath frosting the air in silky grey plumes. They stamped their feet and gazed back with earnest eyes. Gabrielle searched the ground for some grass to feed them, but there was nothing except snow and ice. "Sorry," she said, as she glanced at the saddles resting upon their broad backs. She'd never ridden a horse before, not properly, and she found the idea daunting. But not as daunting as the miles of dark woods and snow between her and the border of Krampusland.

She gazed past the horses toward the far side of the barn. There were three bright shining sleds carefully parked along the back wall. Two of them were painted pine-green but the longest and narrowest was as silver as the moon. It had a steering wheel positioned before a plush padded seat and a control panel with a stick shift and compass in the center. Words were etched in sloping black letters next to the buttons; 'Up', 'Down', 'Go', and 'Stop'. And two words were painted above and below the lever, 'Slow', and 'Fast."

"That seems simple enough." Gabrielle climbed onto the sled and found an 'On' button. She pressed it and jumped as the sled blazed into life with a great roar and a din of clanking gears. Heat filled the barn as a blue flame shot from the back of the craft and scorched the stable wall.

Gabrielle slowly pushed the button marked 'Go', and the sled lurched forward.

The horses neighed and kicked as Gabrielle shot past them and sped across the stable yard toward the fences and a house across the way. The droning runners churned the snow and the sled burst through the gate before Gabrielle jabbed the 'Stop' button, bringing the sled to a halt.

"Okay!" Gabrielle took a moment to catch her breath. She climbed down, closed the stable gate and returned to the sled. She pulled the lever toward slow, pushed the 'Go' button and the craft purred like a cat, its flames melting the snow.

"Oi!"

Three angry looking elves burst from a nearby house, their lanterns bobbing as they ran through the yard. "Stop!"

Gabrielle spun the wheel. The front of the craft turned. She jammed the lever towards 'Fast' and the sled sped on, leaving the elves' irate cries to fade behind her. "Sorry!" Gabrielle called, "I'm in a rush." She shot below the city's arched gate and out along the snowy path.

It was like riding a speedboat through a soft white ocean and the icy air whipped by, biting at her cheeks. Gabrielle pulled her hood down and checked the compass. She turned the wheel until the sled was headed due south. The sled shot across the icy meadow, up a slope, and into a pine forest. She was glad she had the measure of the craft as she yanked the steering wheel left and right while dodging through the trees. They hurtled by, but Gabrielle barely noticed them as she fixed her eyes ahead.

A stump loomed towards her. Gabrielle punched the 'Up' Button and the sled jumped up over the stump and landed hard, the snow exploding around her. And then she was off once more, zipping through the trees, the sled's roar echoing off their trunks.

Gabrielle raced through an elven village nestled deep within the woods. Glowing soft yellow light spilled from windows and bleary eyed faces peered out at her. A pair of elves staggered towards her, their bottles of butterscotch held aloft. Gabrielle spun the wheel, narrowly avoiding them as their squeals and curses colored the air.

"Sorry!" she called. Then the craft broke through the tree line and she sped down a hill towards a great white expanse. It took Gabrielle a moment to realize it was a vast frozen lake. The shifting moonlight turned its surface from white to blue, and then to silver.

A deep, rumble came from the ice below. Gabrielle peered through the gaps in the snow and spotted distant fish. They gazed back with bulbous luminous eyes that didn't look best pleased.

Gabrielle checked her course, she was still heading south. The moon hung white and full above the looming black mountains, their profiles lining the sky like cracked jagged teeth. A hill rose up at the far side of the lake and Gabrielle spotted the dark silhouette of the great pine tree where she'd stood with Krampus. Tiny red and orange lights flickered underneath it. She hoped he had stuck to his word and Percival was there, waiting to be freed.

She pushed the stick-shift as far as it would go. The blue flames roared and the sled shook as it sped across the lake and churned through a bank of snow. The hill drew closer and she could see that the flickering lights were flaming torches.

Gabrielle spotted Krampus's tall, horned silhouette and checked to make sure that the key was still in her pocket. For a moment, she thought about turning around, of racing back to Father Christmas's palace and confessing everything.

Then she pictured Percival waiting for her, the hems of his trousers soaked with snow, his hands clenched and aching from scrubbing the dishes in that dank dark mountain.

Gabrielle's thoughts dissolved as Krampus waved his hands, gesturing for her to stop.

"The wall!" Gabrielle spun the steering wheel and aimed the sled for a rise in the snow and jammed the 'Up' button. The sled hurtled over a rocky slope, taking her flying through the air. The wind whistled in her ears, then she felt something scrape the bottom of the sled and in that moment the wall materialized below her.

Gabrielle sailed through the air, down and down until the sled struck the snow with a mighty crunch and lurched up the hill.

"Move!" Gabrielle shouted as the sled sped through the tangle of trolls, their duffel coats flying as they dived out of her way. T mass of the great dark tree loomed towards her.

Gabrielle jabbed at the 'Stop' button, bringing the sled to a halt inches from the trunk.

"You made it," Krampus clasped his hands and stepped away from a small bonfire near the base of the tree. He gave Gabrielle a devilish grin as he reached out toward her. "The key, if you please. Now."

# CHAPTER TWENTY-SEVEN

Gabrielle hid her revulsion as Krampus's forked tongue slithered from his mouth and caught a floating ember.

He chewed upon it with a thoughtful look. "You do have the key?"

Gabrielle nodded and jumped from the sled. The snow crunched below her boots as she approached the tree.

The tiny horned bird perched on Krampus's shoulder glared at Gabrielle through its beady eyes. "You could have given the key to my little friend." Krampus patted the bird's head. "It would have saved time."

"I didn't trust it."

Krampus continued to smile, but Gabrielle could see the anger in his eyes. "Never mind. All that matters is you're here, and I'm here, and the deal is almost done." He extended his hand. "The key."

Gabrielle glanced around the hill. All she could see were trolls, most of them gathered around the campfire and torches. "Where's my brother?"

Krampus clapped his hands. Madam Grystle stepped out from behind the tree, leading Percival by a chain attached to his wrist. "Gabby!" A weak smile flickered through his bewilderment. "You're here?"

"Don't worry, Perce. We're going home."

"Are you?" Krampus's smile was as hard as flint.

"Yes, I am. You asked me to do something and I did it. Let my brother go."

"I will." Krampus's tail swatted the snow. "Just as soon as you give me my key."

Gabrielle did her best not to show her fear while Madam Grystle stared, her tusks gleaming in the firelight. "I'll give you the key, but you have to let all the children in your mountain go." Gabrielle forced herself to gaze straight into Krampus's fiery yellow and orange eyes.

"That was not a part of our deal." Krampus wagged his finger. "You're old enough to know better, so don't push your luck."

"If you want the key-"

"I said no!" His growl made Gabrielle jump. "The children are mine until I choose to release them. It's a tradition, a law older than I care to remember. *Those who behave are given gifts, those who don't are mine.* Just as you should have been, were it not for whatever sorcery you conceal behind your mask of innocence."

Gabrielle swallowed. She didn't want to test his patience any further or he might well discover the truth about her *sorcerous powers...* She held out the key.

Krampus's eyes blazed as he snatched it and held it up "Good. Very good indeed." He stepped towards her, blocking out the light. "And now, Gabrielle Greene, let's conclude our business. For once and for all."

# CHAPTER TWENTY-EIGHT

"Release the boy, if you will, Madam Grystle," Krampus said.

"Well, I wouldn't. Not if I didn't have to." Madam Grystle squeezed Percival's arms. "He's as skinny as a desert chicken, but there might still be some scraps on his bones that are worth chewing-"

"Release the boy now, Madam Grystle." Krampus's tail lashed the snow. "I'm tired of him. And his sister."

"Such a waste." Madam Grystle unlocked the chains and they fell to the snow. Percival stared at them for a moment, before staggering over to Gabrielle. He wrapped his arms around her with such force they both nearly toppled over.

"It's okay, Perce," Gabrielle whispered, "Let's go home." She turned to face Krampus. "How do we get back?"

"I should let you find your own way. See if you can make it across the frozen miles." Krampus stared at Gabrielle for a moment, before shaking his head. "But despite what they say, I'm no monster. Not for the most part at least. Follow me." He led them across the hill, and Gabrielle gasped as she saw the valley on the other side.

A sea of black tents stood below them and everywhere Gabrielle looked, she saw trolls and sleighs, and campfires. A din of clanging iron rang out and a sled pulled by infernal-looking hounds padded through the snow carrying bundles of swords.

It was a war camp.

Gabrielle felt sick. "What was the key for?" she asked Krampus.

"This key?" Krampus held it up with a toothy grin. "Why, this is the key to Christmas. And now that I own it I can go wherever I please. Even the invisible wall that festive oaf built can't stop me. It's mine," he waved his hands through the air. "All of it's mine."

"I didn't..." A wave of nausea passed through Gabrielle.

"Shhh," Krampus said. "I've had enough of you and your brother to last me an eternity. Go. Return to wherever it is that you belong." He clapped his hands.

The ground beneath Gabrielle's feet rumbled and shuddered. She threw her hands out to steady herself, but it seemed as if the whole world was shaking.

"Enjoy your journey," Krampus called. "And a thousand thanks for all that you have done."

# CHAPTER TWENTY-NINE

"What's-" Gabrielle's words were snatched away as the ground opened and she found herself shooting down a narrow black tunnel. Down and down she went, the ground rushing by at dizzying speed. Percival's muffled screams kept pace with her from somewhere above or below.

It was like riding a flume in a water park, only without the water, as the tunnel snaked this way and that before opening into a black abyss. "Help!" Gabrielle's voice echoed all around her. "Please!" She thumped against a hard flat surface. It felt like sanded brick as the tunnel dipped down and a rush of cold air rose up, slowing her descent.

Light burst up from below and Gabrielle's boots skidded across the hard floor as she tumbled from the opening of a sooty fireplace.

Percival's cry rang out as he landed in a crumpled heap beside her. His face, hair and clothes were coated in ash and soot. As were Gabrielle's.

"What are you doing?" asked a voice.

Gabrielle blinked against the glare of the light. She caught a glimpse of beige walls and a great clock, and she realized where they were. Back in Uncle Florian's living room, sprawled out on the floor in front of the empty grate.

Matilda stood before them with her hands nestled in a pair of oven mitts. Her mouth gaped open, revealing her metal braces. "Have you been up the chimney? You have, haven't you?" Her eyes grew wider as she glanced at the carpet, once russet brown, now peppered with soot. "Father's going to go mad. He can't afford to have this cleaned!"

"What happened?" As Percival rubbed the soot from his eyes, he smeared it deeper into his skin.

"Come on Perce." Gabrielle stood slowly to avoid hitting her head on the chimney breast and helped him to his feet.

"I..." For once Matilda was lost for words as she watched them stride across the carpet. Gabrielle glanced back at their trail of sooty footprints. Almost like footsteps in the snow... she took her boots off and told Percival to do the same. "We'll get washed," Gabrielle said, "and then I'll clean this up as best I can."

"It will never come up." Matilda folded her arms. "And even if it does, I'm still going to tell father what you did."

"You do that." Gabrielle pulled Percival into the hallway and led him to the bathroom. "Go on, get in the shower, Perce."

Percival looked utterly bewildered. "What happened? We were..."

"Somewhere else..." Gabrielle tried to think. A memory flitted through her mind, just out of reach. A fleeting image of a snowy hill with wild looking men in duffel coats. And a tall, furry beast with horns.

Or was he a man?

And the white palace...the memory flickered and then it was gone. Gabrielle shook her head. "Go on Perce." She ushered him through the bathroom door and waited until she heard the water running.

Gabrielle went to her room and stood before the full-length mirror. She didn't recognize the filthy clothes she was wearing. This wasn't her coat, and the boots weren't hers either. She prised the gloves off and glanced through the window. It was late afternoon and the sky was as grey as the melancholia filling her heart.

*Why do I feel so sad? And why do I feel so guilty? Like I've done something terrible...*

The dissolving snowmen in the neighbor's garden looked like mutants as they shed chunks of dingy white snow. The sight of them reminded Gabrielle of something, but she couldn't think what. Ragged limp decorations hung from the rooftops and doors across the way, fluttering weakly in the wind. "What are they for?" Gabrielle murmured. Was someone having a party? She dimly recalled that something was supposed to happen at this time of year, but she couldn't think for the life of her, what.

A calendar hung on her wall. Tiny doorways peppered a landscape of a great black mountain with a pair of rocky horns jutting from its summit. Gabrielle opened one of the little doors and recoiled as a black worm slithered out. "Urgh!"

She stooped down to grab it but it wriggled across the carpet and vanished through a gap near the wainscoting. Gabrielle paused as she took her coat off. She tried desperately to remember what it was she'd forgotten. "We went somewhere..." she said. "But-"

The bathroom door opened and Percival traipsed past her with a towel around his hair. He went to his room and closed the door.

Gabrielle almost called out to him, to see if he could remember...

What?

She shook her head.

Whatever it was, it was gone now.

Gone, with a cold, absent finality.

# CHAPTER THIRTY

The weeks tumbled by in a blur, each day almost identical to the one that preceded it. Every morning brought thick grey skies that slowly but surely grew darker and darker until they merged with the night. The house was cold and everything reeked of damp. Great globs of water streaked the windows as the rain lashed down and the last stubborn chunks of ice melted in the street. And with them, Gabrielle's memory of...something else. Somewhere else. Another place, another world. Gossamer thin dreams of magic, adventure, and terror stirred near the edges of her mind as she awoke each morning, but shattered before she lifted her head from her pillow.

The entire city was under the same miserable curse as the house, but at least going out freed them from Matilda, who hated the drizzly weather. Gabrielle and Percival wandered the streets looking for something to do, but found little.

One morning she ventured into the market square and found it festooned with frayed black bunting and a towering dead tree in a tattered foil bucket. Its spindly limbs were bare and spider-like, and something about the tree made Gabrielle feel desperately sad. Dour-faced tourists haunted the streets, wandering aimlessly with scarcely suppressed irritation. As if they'd been let down or cheated of something. Gabrielle had no idea why anyone would choose to come to such a listless, grave and mournful place as this, and have the nerve to be annoyed.

And then there was that strange beastly figure that stared out from the posters pasted in almost every shop window she passed. A savage looking creature with a long, goat-like face, horns jutting from its furry head and malice bursting from its orange-yellow eyes. Below its toothy wide grin was a message festively printed in several languages:

'Merry Krampusmas! Rejoice - the 25th of December is almost here!'

Gabrielle had no idea what Krampusmas was, or what would happen when it arrived tomorrow, but she had a feeling it wasn't going to be good.

People dressed up as the beastly creature and stood at street corners, leering and handing out lumps of coal. Gabrielle and Percival gave them a wide berth, but now and then one would take them by surprise when it leaped out at them. This unnerved Gabrielle and absolutely terrified Percival. She tried telling him it was just stupid people in stupid outfits, but he seemed doubtful.

As they walked down a narrow street Gabrielle sighed, spotting yet another shop with a big sign across the windows. Even though she couldn't read what it said, its meaning was clear enough. The lights were out, the door locked. Another shop closed. It looked as though it had been a toy shop, and for some strange reason Gabrielle had a notion she'd once wanted to buy something there. But she couldn't remember what. Just that it had been important. Before...

"Urgh!" Percival moaned.

A cold wet raindrop splattered the back of Gabrielle's neck, then the heavens opened and a torrent of rain pounded the street.

"Quick!" Percival grabbed her coat sleeve and led her across the street to a large department store. They made their way through a section of scented candles, wooden whatnots and stainless steel kitchen gadgets to the center of the warm bright store.

A line of children waited in a long solemn line. Gabrielle had never seen such doleful faces. A man in fiery red robes sat in a tall chair before them wearing a mask with long arching horns and a wolfish face. A young boy sat balanced upon his knee, as the man boomed, "Heh, heh, heh."

It's supposed to be *ho ho ho*. Gabrielle had no idea how she knew this, but she did, and she was certain of it.

"Poor kid," Percival said as the costumed creature reached into a sack and pulled out a handful of sweets with twisted black and white wrappers. The boy attempted a grateful smile as he unwrapped one and began to chew. "Bleurgh!" he screwed his eyes up and stuck his tongue out. It was as black as tar.

"Merry Krampusmas!" the masked man hollered.

"I don't like this." Percival said.

"Let's go." Gabrielle dragged Percival through the store but froze as a tiny man leaped out in front of her. He wore a long navy-blue duffel coat, and his wiry black hair spilled from below his hood. He winked with one bone-white eye and laughed, his foul breath coming out in an overwhelming blast that smelled like a heap of damp, sweaty socks.

"Come on Perce." Gabrielle pulled him away. The little man snickered and bowed.

They left the store and ran, through the rain, until they stood beneath their uncle's porch. Gabrielle opened the door, kicked her shoes off, and wandered into the living room. Matilda sat at the table. A pile of sweets was spread out before her, and empty black and white striped wrappers circled her feet like fallen leaves. "Oh, you're back?" As she grimaced, Gabrielle saw her tongue. It was as black as the soot stains upon the carpet.

Gabrielle was about to respond when the front door creaked open behind them and a blast of chilly air passed through the house. Uncle Florian walked slowly into the room. He tried to smile but it fell apart. "I...I had to shut the shop."

"You're home early. Are you back for long?" Matilda glanced at the television, seemingly worried he might disturb the programs she was planning on watching.

"Perhaps. I had to shut the shop," Uncle Florian said again.

"Why?" Matilda asked. "Slow day?"

"It's been a slow year. *Another* slow year," Uncle Florian said. "This should be my busy time. Every December...I used to put up decorations and make magical things that brought customers into the shop. Parents would come in with their children, and they would buy my clocks because I'd make them look special...but I can't remember how. Or why. Not that it matters, because I don't think a single person has been to my shop in the past two weeks, apart from the postman bringing my bills. It's the same everywhere. All the shops are closing asides from the big store. This city is dying." His eyes glinted as he shook his head. "I'm sorry. Never mind me, I'm just tired. I'll go and lie down for a while, get some rest. I'm sure I'll feel better later. " He glanced at Gabrielle and Percival and attempted another smile. "I'm sorry, I know I haven't been around much, but at least I'll have plenty of time to spend with you now."

Matilda waited until her father had left the room, before shooting a furious glare at Gabrielle. "This is your fault."

"How?" Gabrielle asked.

"Everything was fine until you came here," Matilda said. "We had money, and we were happy. We didn't have to share our pizzas, or the bathroom, or anything. Everything's ruined now and it's all your fault. You and your stupid parents. Why can't they sort out their stupid problems and take you back to your stupid country and-"

"Shut up!" Gabrielle's cheeks blazed and for the briefest moment, she felt like her old self. Whatever that was.

Anger and fear passed across Matilda's dumb face. She looked as if she were about to say something, when a rustle came from the chimney. Followed by the sound of scratching nails, a high pitched yell, and a thump.

Gabrielle stared at the fireplace, expecting to find a bird or who knew what sitting in the empty grate.

But there was nothing.

Then a tiny sooty footprint appeared on the carpet, followed by another..

"What are you gawking at?" Matilda demanded. "Did you stuff something up the chimney? Is this another prank?"

"No..." Gabrielle stopped as two red pointed shoes appeared in the soot, they were followed by forest green leggings and a long coat. A pair of bright blue eyes gazed from a long pointed face framed with coppery hair. The little man clapped his hands and the soot rose from his clothes and wafted back up the chimney.

And then he vanished.

"Did you see that?" Gabrielle asked.

"See what?" Matilda coughed and swatted at the sooty air.

"What was it?" Percival's voice was low and grave.

The little man reappeared. He mouthed words as if he were stuck behind a thick pane of glass. Then he curled his hands into fists, his face twisting with frustration as he disappeared again.

"What did you see?" Matilda asked. "Tell me!"

"Nothing. It was just...nothing." Gabrielle grasped Percival's sleeve and led him from the room before Matilda's rage could explode. She walked down the dark hall to her room, and paused as the living room door creaked behind them.

Gabrielle turned back, expecting to see Matilda, but there was no one there.

# CHAPTER
# THIRTY-ONE

Gabrielle shoved her bedroom door closed, annoyed that there was no way to lock it.

"What was it?" Percival asked.

"I don't know."

"Was it a ghost? I don't like ghosts."

Gabrielle jumped as something tugged her sleeve.

Percival was on the other side of the room by the window. His face fell. "What's going on?"

The air flickered as the little man reappeared by the door.

"Can you see him, Percival?" Gabrielle asked.

"I can't see anything. Stop it, Gabs. It's not funny."

I'm seeing things. Gabrielle closed her eyes and willed the hallucination to vanish, and when she opened her eyes, he was gone. "I'm sorry, Percival. I haven't slept well for the last few days. Nothing's going on, I'm just imagining things."

And yet the sight of that little man had sparked something

else, a memory of a time where something seemed to have happened. A mistake that had shaped everything around her. A terrible error that had plunged the city into darkness and invited that fiendish creature that stared out from every shop window.

"It's still raining." Percival pressed his face against the window. "I don't think it's ever going to stop."

And it hadn't been raining before this terrible thing had happened. Gabrielle was certain of it. No it had been... snowing. The thought was followed by a stirring in the air, and as she puzzled over the little man from the chimney, a flood of memories rushed through her mind. "But that was just a dream."

"What are you muttering about?" Percival demanded.

"I don't know." Gabrielle glanced into the garden. It had definitely been white before, she was sure of it. Everything had been white. The memory stirred once more and as she was on the cusp of remembering she realized it might be better to let the memory go, let it just wilt away. If she didn't... there would be consequences. "But I can't. It happened."

"What happened?" Percival asked. "Stop being weird. I don't like it."

"Christmas happened!"

The little man reappeared standing on Gabrielle's bed, staring her in the face. He rolled his eyes and mouthed, "Finally," before pulling an ornate silver flask from his pocket. He unscrewed the lid and curling wisps of steam wafted up along with the unmistakable aroma of hot chocolate. He held the flask out to Gabrielle and his eyes bulged as he slowly mouthed the word 'drink'. He looked like a goldfish. A wizened, angry goldfish.

Gabrielle shook her head.

He narrowed his eyes before taking a sip. He wiped the

top of the flask with his sleeve and held it out to Gabrielle. 'Drink', he mouthed again. The warm rich scent stirred her ghostly memories and Gabrielle reached out for the flask and took a sip.

"Finally!" the man said, and she heard him. "Give your brother some so he can hear me too. What I have to say affects everyone here."

"I'm not giving Percival a drop until you tell me what's in it."

Percival stared at Gabrielle as if she'd lost her mind.

The little man shrugged. "It's just a restorative. A memory potion. You humans are beyond forgetful."

"How do I know its not-"

"What? Poisoned? If it was poisoned I wouldn't be talking to you, would I? I'd be rolling around on the floor going blue in the face. You've had some and you're still alive, aren't you? We don't have much time. Give your brother the flask."

Gabrielle passed the flask to Percival. "Drink it. Just a sip."

"Where did you get that?" Percival held the flask up. "What's going on?"

"Just drink it, Percival. It's perfectly fine. I think. I hope."

Percival looked doubtful, but took a swig all the same. His eyes grew bright and wide as he gazed at the little man. "Who's that?"

"It's alright, Perce."

"But where-"

"Can you hear me?" the little man asked.

Gabrielle suddenly recognized his droll voice, and with that recognition came a new flood of memories. A train passing through dark, snowy lands, a black mountain and a horned beast within its murky caverns. An invisible wall and a key from... *"Christmas!"* Gabrielle said, and now she recognized the little man. "Stark!"

"Finally." Stark looked at Gabrielle as if she were a most ridiculous creature. "You remember now."

"Yes. I-"

"Stole Christmas. Or as good as."

"No,' Gabrielle said. "I didn't. I just took an old key. So I could get Percival back." She looked away as a blush warmed her cheeks.

"That *old key* was the key to Christmas, and you gave it to Krampus." Stark gestured to the rain pouring down the window. "How are you enjoying Krampusmas by the way?"

"Krampusmas?" Percival asked.

"That's what he's calling it," Stark said. "Hardly the most original name, is it? But he has the key, and therefore the holiday, so he can call it whatever he likes. He's taken the palace and everything around it." He blinked rapidly and wiped his eyes with the back of his hand. "The master's gone. He relented. Gave up."

"Where is he?" Gabrielle asked.

"Hiding in the mountains like a common criminal. It's so undignified."

"Who's hiding?" Percival asked.

"Father Christmas," Gabrielle said.

"No way!" Percival's eyes widened. "Really?"

"Really," Gabrielle said. "I stole his key and gave it to Krampus. It was the only way I could get you back, Perce."

Stark glared at Gabrielle, but slowly his face softened. "I suppose you didn't intend for any of this to happen, and what's done is done. But I can't bear to give up, not while there's still a chance. " His eyes found Gabrielle's. "Will you help me? Please."

"How?" Gabrielle asked. "I can't fight Krampus! The only reason he couldn't get me on Krampus night was because I hadn't done anything wrong. I just took the blame for the bad things other kids did."

"Why?" Percival asked.

"Because I needed money."

"What for?"

Gabrielle shrugged. "I wanted to...do something...but it doesn't matter now. The shop's closed and Christmas is gone."

"It doesn't have to be," Stark said. "There's still time. But the clock's ticking."

"But what can I do?" Gabrielle said.

"You stood up to Krampus once," Stark replied, "do it again."

"But I didn't, not really. He thought I was a sorceress, but I'm not."

"You still bested him," Stark said. "And he still thinks you have powers, that's why he wiped your memory and sent you back here. You might have pretended a lot of things, Miss Greene, but you're still braver than most who have faced him."

"I'm sorry, I can't go back."

"You really stole the key to Christmas?" Percival asked. Gabrielle nodded. "Is that why Christmas is gone?"

"Not only gone, it's as if it never existed," Stark added.

"I want it back," Percival said. He gave Stark an earnest look. "I'll help you."

"We're not going back." Gabrielle folded her arms.

"I am," Percival said.

"You're not going anywhere, it's too dangerous. Krampus is a monster."

"I know that," Percival said. "He locked me up under that mountain, didn't he? Which means I owe him." Percival stood beside Stark. "Let's go."

"Percival!" Gabrielle said.

"No," Percival mirrored her by folding his arms. "You treat me like I'm a baby, but I'm not. I was the one stuck in that mountain with all those other kids. I was the one who had to scrub all of those filthy dishes and pull all those hairs from the drains. And worse. Krampus stole me away, I'm not letting him take Christmas too."

Gabrielle was about to send Percival to his room, but he was right, and she knew it. How many times had she asked him to toughen up and look out for himself? And now he was. *I can't steal that from him.* Gabrielle clenched her fists. "Okay. But if anything happens to my brother..."

"He'll stand up for himself," Stark said. "Now, let's go." His gaze fell upon the advent calendar with the great black mountain and the hidden doorways filled with slithering worms. "Another one of Krampus's abominations. Well, it'll be the first thing we take back. And we can use it as our portal back to Christmas."

Stark pulled a stick from his pocket. A silver star was tethered to the end with a length of purple string. Showers of bright golden embers spilled from it as he waved it through the air. The sparkling light swept over the advent calendar and as it glimmered, the painted black mountain began to change. Slowly, a new mountain appeared. This one topped with billowy snow that looked like scoops of ice cream and a jolly full moon smiled as it floated among the twinkling stars. It winked at Gabrielle and Percival, before vanishing behind a snowy peak.

"Perhaps you can find the door to Christmas Eve," Stark said to Percival. Percival kneeled down and ran a finger across the calendar. His fingers stopped at the edge of a tiny door in the mountain's summit. "Found it!"

"Open it, if you will," Stark said.

Bright amber light burst from the opening, filling the room with a magical glow as flurries of snow wafted in with the crisp fresh air. Gabrielle caught a glimpse of blue sky and of a forest of chocolate-brown trees.

"There, a way into Christmas" Stark said. "and with far less soot than that blasted chimney." He rubbed his tiny hands together as an icy wind blew in from the little open door. "Fetch your coats and gloves. Wrap up warm."

Gabrielle rifled through her wardrobe and found the clothes Krampus's tailor had given her. She pulled them on. Percival waddled from his room like a stuffed penguin, wearing two jumpers beneath his coat, and a thick red scarf. "Come on then," Percival said. "Let's go get Christmas."

# CHAPTER
# THIRTY-TWO

Gabrielle stepped from her dingy carpet onto the fresh drift of snow. It crunched below her boots and the wind brought a rich scent of pine and a sprinkling of snowflakes from the tree branches. She pulled her scarf snug around her neck.

"Wow!" Percival stumbled through the door, his eyes growing wide as he glanced around the forest. Gabrielle caught one last glimpse of her gloomy bedroom, as Stark slammed the door behind him.

"Can we get back?" Gabrielle did her best to keep her tone light. She'd been a different person the last time she was here. *The wickedest girl in the city.* Or so everyone said, and that title had made her feel strong and fearsome, and determined. But it wasn't how she felt now. She was just plain old Gabrielle Greene once more, and standing in this place made her feel small and exposed.

"That door only goes one way. There are other ways back, but we can't concern ourselves with that now. We've work to do." Stark pulled branches from a nearby tree, softly apologizing as he did so. He stripped the bark with his knife and laid them upon the snow. Then he pulled out his wand and waved it over the branches until they transformed into skis with bindings of woven white bark. "Tie them on tightly." Stark threaded his pointed shoes through the straps and secured them into place. Gabrielle and Percival did the same.

"And now for, ah yes, here we are." Stark reached into a small bushy tree and carefully removed three pine cones. "Take one." He handed a cone to Percival and the moment he took it, it glowed with a bright sunny-yellow light.

Gabrielle's turned from nutty brown to bright silver, then it felt warm and as light as air.

Stark's cone burst into a deep shade of scarlet as he held it aloft. "Onwards!" he said, and then he shot across the snow as if pulled by an invisible rope. "Follow me," he called.

Percival held up his cone. "Onwards!" he called, and cried out in surprise as his makeshift skis jerked forwards. A tremor passed through Gabrielle's cone as she held it into the air and before she finished uttering the word she found herself swooshing over the snow.

"Faster!" Stark called as he slalomed through the trees, sending great clouds of snowflakes rushing up behind him.

"Faster!" Gabrielle shouted. The forest became a blur as she sped forward, heading straight for a pair of trees. She jumped between them and landed with a crunch. They sped along, swishing through the woodland and leaping over logs, until the forest thinned. A great white expanse opened up before them, stretching up to the summit of a hill. The wind battered against Gabrielle but she kept pace with Stark as he raced to the top.

He stopped at the crest of the hill and his face fell. Stark gave Gabrielle a grave look as she drew up beside him. An immense black palace jutted up through the elven forests, its jagged turrets and towers reaching high into the air. Tents and tiny glowing fires encircled the great city walls and a pair of colossal black horns sprawled out from the highest tower, lancing the low flying clouds. The palace was almost unrecognizable, and Gabrielle felt a sad longing for what it had been when she'd last seen it. The palace of Christmas.

"Once, it was called Christmas." Stark's tone was bitter. "Now it's called Krampus. Just like everything else."

"This is my fault." Gabrielle swallowed. "I'm-"

"Regret is as useful to us now as a paper hat in a hailstorm," Stark said. "My master knew, and yet he allowed you to take the key. You do realize that, don't you?"

"Why?"

"Guilt, I suppose. Resignation." Stark gave a bitter smile. "But it's not my tale to tell."

"Where is he?" Gabrielle asked.

Stark pointed to a nearby mountain. "There. But that last vestige will soon fall to Krampus and once it does, it will truly be the end of everything that was."

The peak was as bent and crooked as a witch's hat. Storm clouds, dark and bruised, swirled down over its slopes. "Those clouds are an ill omen. This is not good," Stark said. "Not good at all. We need to go before the storm breaks!" He held his pine cone up. "Onwards!" The cone glowed in the gathering gloom as he swept up the hill and his skis churned the freshly fallen snow. Gabrielle and Percival followed, racing up towards the mountain as the swell of clouds grew all around.

The temperature dropped, and an ominous energy

charged the air. Distant figures climbed the peak. Gabrielle spotted polar bears and snow people, fleeing towards the cave in the side of the mountain. The entrance grew larger as they approached, yawning open like a dark mouth. Long jagged icicles hung down like teeth, and tiny lights flickering in the back of the cavernous throat.

"What is this place?" Percival shouted, his voice trembling as he sped after Stark.

"It's what remains of our secret grottos!" Stark called. "But now its the last refuge of Christmas." He shot through the cave and swept past a pair of lumbering bears. Gabrielle felt the ground tremble below their mighty paws and she flinched as she flew past them, expecting they might lash out with their claws. The icy ground dipped down and she gasped as it took them soaring into the gloom.

The cave walls twinkled with strings of tiny lights as they followed Stark around a bend. His voice echoed back to them, "Slow!"

"Slow," Gabrielle called in response, and the pine cone dimmed and flashed, as she leaned into the bend. "Slow!" Percival called behind her.

Gabrielle turned the corner and called "Stop!" Stark stood before a large wall of gleaming frosty blue and white ice. He carefully placed his pine cone in his pocket. "Keep them safe, in case we need them again." Then he removed his skis and leaned them against the wall of the tunnel. Gabrielle did the same and shivered as she and Percival joined him before the icy door. Stark placed his hand upon its center and whispered, "Forever Christmas!"

It rumbled and a dusting of snow fell from the ceiling as the door opened onto a vast cavern filled with sparkling white lights. They stepped inside and the door slid shut behind them with a mighty thump.

A great bonfire blazed in the center. Elves and bears stood

around it, drinking from tankards and gazing desolately into the flames. It was a terribly melancholy scene. The snow people gathered near the shadowy cavern walls, as far from the fire as they could get. One large snow woman with a mane of gleaming white hair, shot Gabrielle a sour look. As did the polar bear in the knitted woolen suit and the gnomes perched upon the barrel beside her.

Yes, Gabrielle thought, It's me. *The thief of Christmas.*

"Never mind them." Stark sniped as he led them through the cavern toward a large wooden door. He rapped his knuckles against it until a low, weary voice called, "Enter."

The room was small and cozy, its wooden walls decked with sprigs of holly and a fireplace. Father Christmas sat before it, gazing into the flames. His little wooden chair didn't look half as comfortable as the one he'd had in his palace. He offered them a half smile, and apart from her Uncle Florian, Gabrielle couldn't remember seeing such a desolate looking man.

"Are you..." Percival looked awestruck as he gazed up at Father Christmas, who seemed to brighten under his gaze.

Father Christmas strode towards him and offered a hand. "Indeed." He shook Percival's hand. "Unless I'm mistaken, you're Miss Greene's brother, Percival. Ho ho ho. I've seen you before of course."

"When?"

"Every year, about this time." Father Christmas nodded to the red and white trimmed sack leaning against the wall. "If only I had something for you, but I'm afraid it's empty." His eyes twinkled in the firelight as he turned to Gabrielle. "I didn't ask you to come, but I'm thankful you did." He gave Stark a reproachful look, before adding. "I suppose we could do with some cheer in these dark times."

""I'm sorry." Gabrielle said. "I saw what Krampus did to your palace. It looks like something out of a nightmare."

"Quite," Father Christmas said. "As do the lands around it. He's changed everything, save for this mountain. But it won't be long before his shadow falls here, so you must return to your world, before it's too late. Take them back, Stark. Please."

"I brought them here for a reason," Stark said. "They've got strength. We have none."

Gabrielle shook her head. "I wouldn't-"

"You are strong. And resourceful. And more courageous than either of us," Stark said. "You survived Krampus. As did your brother. He suffered greatly at that monster's hands, and yet I haven't heard him complain about it once. You're both strong. That's what we need. Strength." He gave Father Christmas an equally reproachful look. "You cannot give up, Master. Not now." Stark swept his hand towards the door. "This nightmare's affecting everyone, and you let it happen. Now's the time to fix things. We must take action before it's too late."

"Why did you let it happen? Why did you let Krampus take everything?" Gabrielle glanced at Father Christmas.

He peered down past his belly, as if searching for his shoes. "I let you take the key. But only because it was his by right. Not that it should have been. I should never have..." he stopped, and gave a long, low sigh.

"If you tell us what happened we might be able to help you," Percival said.

"Sit." Father Christmas gestured to the chairs around a wooden table in the center of the room. "Sit, and I'll tell you the whole sorry story. For what it's worth."

# CHAPTER THIRTY-THREE

"The night it happened was as dark and cold as this one," Father Christmas said. "Krampus sent his trolls to escort me to the hill that borders our lands. Which is where I played a game of chance, and lost Christmas."

"Why?" Gabrielle asked, her tone more pointed than she'd intended.

"Because I was indebted to Krampus, he lent me his gold and I was unable to pay him back. Gambling seemed like the only way out. We played a round of cards and when I lost he demanded the key to Christmas as payment. What I actually gave him was the key to my pantry, then I fled to my palace before he realized what I'd done. But I knew he'd come after me so I used my remaining powers to conjure an invisible wall. It was the best way I could think of keeping him at bay. And it worked. For a time at least."

Father Christmas continued his story, and by the time he finished, he was slumped in his seat.

"So you and Krampus weren't always enemies?" Percival asked.

"We're two sides of the same coin. Shade and light. I'm the carrot, and he's the stick. Behave and you get a wish, misbehave and you face punishment and toil beneath his mountain. He is what he is, and I am what I am, and we were allies for the most part. That's why I turned to him when I needed the gold. But I never considered how I'd repay it, until it was too late. And that was entirely my fault."

"So you cheated him?" Percival asked.

"Cheated..." Gabrielle's mind whirred She dug into her coat pocket. You can have that card if you like. *Keep it as a souvenir, and a reminder that I always win. Every single time.*" Is this one of the cards you played with?" Gabrielle held up the card and the joker on the front tipped its fool's hat and bowed.

"Yes," Father Christmas said. "How did you come across it?"

"It's from Krampus's laboratory." Gabrielle handed it to Father Christmas and the joker transformed himself into a particularly regal looking Queen of Spades.

"The cards were enchanted." Father Christmas's face reddened. "He cheated me!"

"You cheated too." Percival folded his arms. "You gave him the key to your pantry"

"Yes, but I *had* to," Father Christmas said, "Christmas isn't mine to give away."

"You should talk to him and try to sort this out," Gabrielle said. "Because you're both in the wrong."

"No," Father Christmas shook his head. "It's out of the question. I cannot talk to Krampus. If I were to go anywhere near him, he'd clap me in chains and throw me into his darkest dungeon. That's why I turned a blind eye when you came for the key. I knew I couldn't give it to him, but if someone stole it and gave it to him...well, after that, I just hoped it would all be over."

"It *is all over*," Stark said, as he woke from his snooze, stretched, and leaped down from his chair. "We've lost everything."

"Unless we do something about it," Gabrielle added.

"Impossible! You've seen what Krampus has done to my palace," Father Christmas said. "You've seen his army. The trolls, the Christmas Cat, Madam Grystle..." He shivered.

"If I stole the key once," Gabrielle said, "maybe I can steal it again."

A glimmer of hope shone in Father Christmas' eyes, until he shook his head once more. "I don't know..."

"I'll help her," Percival said.

"As will I," Stark added. "You should stay here, Master, defend the grotto. There's a storm raging out there. And soon it will be joined by another one: Krampus."

Father Christmas nodded. "I'll try and hold them off. Take my sleigh, it's fast. Just be careful." He looked doubtful, as if he wanted to join them. But then the fear in his eyes returned and he nodded for them to leave.

"This way," Stark opened a hidden door in the wall and led Gabrielle and Percival down a long winding tunnel. It twisted and turned before opening into a tiny cavern that looked out on the valley below. The cold winds howled and snowflakes filled the air. Gabrielle gaped at the approaching storm as Stark ran to the corner of the cave and drew back a blanket, revealing a huge sleigh. Its runners were berry-red, its body forest green. A wingback seat rose up from the center and behind it was an open compartment with an empty red sack draped over the edge.

"Wait here." Stark dashed away. Moments later he returned, leading six reindeer.

"Is...is this *the* sleigh?" Percival asked.

"Indeed." As Stark harnessed up the reindeer, their ears twitched and they regarded Gabrielle and Percival with deep black eyes. Gabrielle held her hand out to one of them and it inclined its head, allowing her to pet it.

"And we're really going to ride in his sleigh?" Percival asked, his voice trembling slightly.

"We are. Now climb aboard." Stark pulled out his wand and lit the lanterns that were mounted on the front of the sleigh. Then he hopped up into the chair, gathered up the reins and patted the seat. Gabrielle and Percival sat down beside him and then they were off.

The reindeer cantered through the cave and sped down the side of the mountain. As they raced along the short narrow strip of land they leaped up, carrying the sleigh up and away into the swirling snow.

# CHAPTER
# THIRTY-FOUR

The reindeer galloped up through the air while the snow storm swirled all around them. "Hang on, Perce" Gabrielle shouted as the sleigh rocked and swayed in the wind. She grabbed the railing and peered over the side. Far below, figures trudged up the hill; snow people, gnomes, bears and elves braving the blizzard together.

The dark palace loomed with its black and curled spires like giant spider legs reaching from the depths of the earth. Smoky coal fires flickered in the clearings beyond the city walls and figures huddled around them.

Trolls.

Hundreds of trolls.

"We'll have to land in the forest if we want to be stealthy. Hold tight!" Stark shouted above the screaming gusts of wind.

"How am I going to get past all those trolls?" Gabrielle asked.

"We'll need an army to distract them!" Percival said.

"It would be nice if we had one, Perce." Gabrielle tried her best to mask her irritation. "But we don't."

A slow smile passed across Percival's lips and a gleam lit his eyes. "Then we'll have to make one."

. . .

"Are you sure you want to do this?" Gabrielle asked Percival, as they peered through the trees at the edge of the forest. She shivered as she caught a glimpse of the Christmas Cat slinking through the sea of black tents. It crouched, thrashing its tail and with one brash sweep it sent a pair of trolls flying into the snow. Then it turned and bared its mighty teeth, its eyes flashing with displeasure as the terrified trolls scrambled to their feet and fled.

The city wall loomed over the makeshift camps, encircling the palace with a mighty barrier of sheer black stone. Infernal red lights blazed in all but the highest windows of the towers, and Gabrielle's heart raced when she realized Krampus was behind one of them, lurking with his coterie of monsters.

"It's a truly horrific sight, isn't it." Stark said, his voice carrying a slight tremble. "Why are we doing this? It's madness."

"Because we have to!" Percival whispered. "To save Christmas!" He glanced at the empty sack in the back of the sleigh and turned to Stark. "You can do magic, right?"

"I can conjure. Within reason," Stark replied.

"Good." Percival's face was rapt with concentration.

Gabrielle felt a rush of warmth and pride for her brother as he glared at the palace with defiance, determination, and not a little fear. She wanted to hug him but stopped herself as he took a long breath and began to lay out his plan.

. . .

"Okay, it looks like you and Stark are nearly finished here, Perce" Gabrielle said, "and it's getting dark. I'm going for the key. I'll see you soon." She ducked low and ran through the trees, slowing near the camps to search for an area with the least number of tents between herself and the city wall. And then she waited. "Come on Perce," she whispered, "you can do this."

. . .

"I'm sick of that cat!" Fingledrum growled as the Christmas Cat sat before the fire, its silhouette like a small hill. A small hill with hideously sharp teeth, razor sharp claws, and a thrashing tail that could upend a boat.

Fingledrum dusted the snow from his rough woolen coat and helped his brother, Zarackmish to his feet. Zarackmish's face turned ashen as he gazed into the forest.

"What's wrong?" Fingledrum demanded. And then he followed his brother's gaze toward the trees.

Flashing lights fizzled and sparked among the branches, illuminating a line of squat, thickset figures. They stood perfectly still while firecrackers burst around them. Then, two tiny figures slipped past the motionless battalion and stood before them. "Lay down your weapons!" one called out like a commander, but it sounded very much like a young boy.

"Do as he says and you'll be spared!" the other announced, with the shrill voice of a highfalutin elf.

Fingledrum glanced about to see whether his fellow trolls were aiming to attack or run. He hoped it would be the former, but not one warty hand tightened upon its ax handle, and not one dagger was drawn. Even the Christmas Cat had scarpered, during the very first round of explosions no doubt.

I must *seize the initiative,* Fingledrum thought, *then, when the tale of this great battle is told, my name and brave deeds will ring in Krampus's ears.* He raised his ax in the air and stepped forward. "Charge!" he cried.

The trolls surged as one, the snow high around their knees as they rushed forward. They halted as another round of explosions rang out, and flares of light burst before them. Fingledrum caught sight of the two tiny figures fleeing behind the army. "That's it you cowards, run!" he shouted, as he shook his ax, hoping the rest of their army would follow suit. But they stood defiantly so Fingledrum thrust his ax in the air and charged.

He began to slow as he reached the silent army, and now he realized why they were motionless.

They were snowmen.

But not real living snowmen, these were strange crude figures made of snow with branches and twigs for swords.

Then Fingledrum caught sight of reindeer and a sleigh slipping through the trees. "We've been tricked!" Fingledrum swung his ax and lopped the head off the nearest snowman. It thudded to the ground, its stone eyes staring out above its wide, mocking grin.

"What was the point?" Fingledrum asked, as the other trolls lowered their weapons with relief and disappointment. But as he turned back towards the city, he spotted a small, agile figure crouched upon the top of the wall. It turned his way, before leaping down over the other side, and vanishing into the night.

# CHAPTER
# THIRTY-FIVE

Gabrielle perched on the wall and watched as the trolls charged towards the line of snowmen. It had taken Stark the best part of an hour to conjure the roughly shaped army -the same army now having their snowy heads and limbs lopped off as the humiliated trolls vented their anger at having been duped.

Gabrielle just hoped Percival and Stark escaped before the illusion broke. And that they'd be where they were supposed to be when the time came.

Because if they weren't... Gabrielle shook off the grim thought as she scaled down the wall and jumped into the bank of snow. She ran along the shadowy base of the wall steering clear of the trolls with flaming torches and lanterns that bobbed through the streets. They roared and sang songs of glorious conquests, the sound grating and discordant, but at least it helped Gabrielle keep track of where they were. She slipped from alley to alley, until she found herself alongside the palace.

It was even more hideous close up, a menacing behemoth of black stone and eerie flickering lights, that stood in brutal contrast to the gleaming ice cream colored palace it had once been.

Gabrielle placed her gloves against the wall, and climbed, one hand after the other as she worked her boots into the crevices and joints. The higher she climbed, the fiercer the wind roared and battered her face with snow. Gabrielle narrowed her eyes and fought to keep her bearings.

The climb was so much harder than it had been before, and she had to force herself to contain her rising panic and doubt. She focused on reaching for the window gleaming beside her but gasped as she spotted trolls in the room, just beyond the glass. They stood by a fire, knocking tankards together and slopping their drinks over the carpet. Their songs were reminiscent of Christmas carols but sung in a strange language, their tone vicious and mocking.

Gabrielle continued, shimmying up toward the arched, latticed window above. Her heart lurched as she let go of the wall with one hand, and pulled at the bottom rail of the window. It opened a fraction and then stuck. "Please!" she squealed as she tugged sharply on the cold metal rail and almost lost her footing.

It jerked opened. Gabrielle placed her shaking hands on the sill, pulled herself up and tumbled onto the plushly carpeted floor. The wind whistled like a kettle behind her and snow fluttered into the room. Gabrielle reached out and closed the window as softly as she could.

The chamber was different but it was definitely the same room she had been in before. The walls were black now, and punctuated with carved stone monograms of 'K' contained by thorny swirling vines. Eerie blue flames danced in the fireplace and a bas-relief sculpture of Krampus's head was mounted above it, encircled by thick rusted chains.

A woman's voice drifted in from the antechamber. She was singing in a harsh, flat tone and failing to hold a tune. "Bones, bones, and despicable things, peacock hearts and beetle wings. Maggots, spiders, louse and fleas, rancid fat and buttered peas."

"Madam Grystle," Krampus's voice boomed from the room beyond, "I want my soup and I want it now. As thick as tar and as cold as the grave."

"Great art cannot be hurried. Now be patient, it's almost ready," she replied.

Gabrielle tip-toed to the doorway of the antechamber and peeked inside. It had been fashioned into a makeshift kitchen. A stove laden with bubbling pots and pans stood against the wall next to a huge black cauldron. Madam Grystle leaned over it, dropping cups of snow and ice into its dark depths. "Cold as the grave, he says," she muttered. "This broth should be piping hot. But who am I to argue? I've only been cooking for more centuries than...than I care to count."

In the room beyond, Gabrielle could see Krampus framed by a blazing furnace. His feet rested upon a stool as he leaned back in his chair and munched bright fiery coals from a bucket upon his lap. Something upon his chest gleamed in the firelight.

The key?

"Don't fill up on that coal," Madam Grystle called. "You'll lose your appetite."

Krampus replied with a mighty burp. Embers flew from his mouth and twinkled around his head. He caught each of them with his forked tongue, then he set the coal bucket on a table and leaned back in his chair.

*It's now or never.* Gabrielle's heart thumped hard as she sneaked into the antechamber, and hugged the wall opposite Madam Grystle's cauldron. She clamped the sleeve of her coat over her nose to combat the pervasive stench of rot, and watched as Madam Grystle dropped what looked like pureed goldfish into the cauldron. The ogress's tusks gleamed as she grinned and stirred the foul brew with a giant wooden spoon.

Gabrielle crept by, one tentative step at a time. She had almost reached the door, when her sleeve caught a vase of withered flowers that sat upon a stand.

It slipped and fell. Gabrielle threw her hands out and grabbed it before it could smash upon the floor. She gagged as the flower's petals opened, releasing a stench of decaying rat.

Gabrielle was so close to the furnace room that she could feel the burning heat, and her heart almost stopped as a loud belch burst from Krampus with a roar like a contained explosion. "Excuse me," he muttered. As he stretched his legs out, Gabrielle saw that his cloven hooves weren't resting on a stool at all, they were propped up on the back of a crouching troll. The creature's eyes were closed, and it seemed by the sound of muffled snores that it was fast asleep.

She edged through the door as Krampus lay back, humming and staring up at the ceiling. The master of his realm and lord of his manor.

"I hope you're hungry," Madam Grystle called from the antechamber. "The broth is almost ready. There's just one more ingredient to add. Once it's been restrained."

Time was running out. Gabrielle summoned the last frayed threads of her courage and stole across the room, keeping her gaze upon the gleaming chain around Krampus's neck.

She rose up from behind his chair, and reached over the tangled, matted fur on the back of his neck. Gabrielle almost had the clasp open when he spluttered and a blast of embers flew from his mouth.

"Do you need a drink of water?" Madam Grystle called from the other room.

"Yes! Quickly!" As he leaned over and coughed again, Gabrielle unhooked the clasp. But as she grabbed the chain, he whirled round and caught her hand. Shock and fury lit his eyes. "You!" he roared. "The girl who would steal Christmas. Again!" His tongue lashed through the air like the crack of a whip. "Thief!"

Gabrielle reached down and gave his wrist a savage twist. He roared, released her hand and kicked the troll resting under his hooves as he clambered to his feet. Gabrielle was almost through the antechamber when Madam Grystle leaped out to block her path.

"Don't you move!" Madam Grystle squinted with fury as Gabrielle danced to the left. The ogress reached out, grabbed Gabrielle by the waist and lifted her up, crushing the air from her lungs.

Krampus thundered in from his chamber, his sleepy-eyed troll close behind. "Keep the verminous child still," he commanded.

Gabrielle tried to squirm from Madam Grystle's grasp, but she had her firmly in her grip. "Get off!" Gabrielle thrust her foot back and felt the heel of her boot gouge Madam Grystle's shin. The ogress gave a savage cry but held her firm. Gabrielle kicked harder, Madam Grystle dropped her and fell back, tumbling into her cauldron with a great splosh.

With a rush of smoky hot air Krampus's claws sliced towards her. She bolted from the room, focusing on the window ahead as she hoped with all her heart that Percival was there.

Because if he wasn't...

"Stop!" Krampus boomed.

Gabrielle grabbed the window and threw it open. She climbed out onto the ledge.

His hairy fingers seized her foot. She kicked back and heard a crunch, before she toppled out.

"Perrrrrrrrrrrrrcccciiivvvaaaaaalllllllll!"

The wind howled as she fell, the snowy white ground rising up at a terrible rate. The roofs of the houses below raced up as she rushed towards the ground. Something moved in the blurred periphery of her vision, and then the air was knocked from her chest and she plunged into a billowy mound of furs.

The reindeers kicked the air and the sleigh wooshed down an alleyway behind the shops and houses.

"Are you okay?" Percival called, as Stark pulled the reins and the magical deer took them up over the city wall. They plunged down amongst the tents and shot across the snow, scattering trolls like skittles.

"I got the key." Gabrielle held it up. Percival gave an excited cry while Stark extended his sincerest congratulations.

"We did it!" Percival said. "We saved Christmas!"

Gabrielle was about to cheer and throw her arms around him when Percival glanced behind her and his face turned ashen white.

# CHAPTER THIRTY-SIX

Krampus's great black sled was closing in behind them, his wolves sprinting through the sky. He glared at Gabrielle, his fiery eyes scorching the air between them as the menacing sleigh thumped down and plowed through the snow like the fin of a great black shark. Krampus stood with his hands taut upon the reins and howled, his forked tongue lashing the air.

"Go faster!" Percival shouted.

Stark shook the reins. The reindeer dashed forward and the sleigh hurtled through the trees at dizzying speeds. Gabrielle grabbed a branch and pulled it free. She hurled it at Krampus. It bounced off his horns and he roared with rage.

Inch by inch his wolves gained on them and she watched in horror as he held up his clawed fist and pulled it down.

Thick chunks of snow and ice rained down upon her and everything turned white. She wriggled free just in time to see a large tree trunk looming ahead through the powdery snow. Stark pulled at the reins and the reindeer swerved sharply while the tree whizzed by in a blur.

They sped on, racing up the hill and bounding over logs and stumps. Gabrielle and Percival grasped the railings to stop themselves tumbling from the sleigh.

"Yes, hold on tight," Stark called out, "we're going up!" He whistled and the reindeer shot up through the snow-laden boughs.

The moon was huge and full as they sailed through the sky towards the crest of the hill. Gabrielle's heart lurched as she glanced back. Krampus's wolves careered behind them, black blurs upon a white backdrop. The wind shrieked in her ears and she jolted forwards as their sleigh bounced into the snow.

Gabrielle grasped the rail of the sleigh with one hand, and the back of Percival's coat with the other as she looked back. Krampus's sleigh had lost ground on them but her smile faded when he raised his fist and flicked his fingers apart. The ground rumbled.

"No!" Stark cried.

A huge rock erupted from the ground.

Directly in their path.

Stark pulled the reins, but it was too late. The reindeer galloped over it, their hooves slipping on the icy stone. They slid and tumbled, overturning the sleigh. It creaked and groaned as it careened onto its side and the sky and ground spun around and around.

Gabrielle found herself flying, and for the briefest of moments everything was slow, white and perfectly serene. She floated among the snowflakes that drifted around her and all was silent.

Then with a crude harsh shock she struck the ground.

She tried to cry out, but the wind had been knocked from her lungs. A wailing rush rang in her ears as metal and wood squealed over the rock. Krampus's wolves flew over her turning the world black and with a mighty whump, his sleigh crashed down beside her.

A whip-crack of pain shot through her as she sat up and wrapped her arms around her chest.

His wolves growled, their ragged breath frosting the air as Krampus towered above them clutching birch sticks in his fist. The devilish, charming rogue was gone now, his crooked smile replaced with a snarl. "I'll beat you as black as coal and as blue as ice."

Gabrielle stumbled to her feet and stood between Krampus and Percival. "Listen-"

"Let's see your magic now, girl. Let's see what you've got. Other than deception and lies," Krampus spat a gob of molten fire that hissed and sizzled in the snow. "Give me my key, or by everything below the rock and stone, I'll thrash you into the middle of next week." Firelight danced in his eyes. "Give it back!"

Gabrielle clutched the key defiantly but winced as he raised his birch sticks.

She heard them whizz through the air and felt the breeze descending towards her. Gabrielle flinched.

But the blow never came.

She opened her eyes to see a pudgy white hand grasping Krampus's wrist, the sticks inches from her face.

"You will not strike her!"

"Get off me!" Krampus snatched his wrist away from Father Christmas.

Father Christmas's face softened. "We need to end this feud here and now. I know everything. I know how you cheated me, and-"

"Cheated *you!*" Krampus snarled. "You lost the bet and failed to pay the stakes. You cheated me, then ran away to hide in your lair like a plump spider. All of this is mine." He swept his birch sticks through the air. "All of it. So tell the girl to hand over my key or I'll thrash the lot of you."

Father Christmas dug into his robes and pulled out the playing card Gabrielle had given him. "The deck was loaded." He let the card go. It soared past Krampus's head and was snatched up by the howling wind. "You didn't win, you duped me. Now return to your realm and leave me to mine."

"Tell me," Krampus said, "just what will you do with this empire of yours? Because it seems to me that you gave up on it years ago." His eyes strayed to Father Christmas's belly. "You grew lazy and complacent, built a machine to do everything for you. Is that the lowly value you place on your position? You're a lost cause, Nicholas. One big, fat joke."

"Yes," Father Christmas said, "I was wrong, tired. But now I'm waking up. Believe me."

"Are you? You sound so high and mighty now, but don't forget what you stole from me. You took my gold with no intention of paying it back." Krampus shot a venomous glance at Gabrielle. "She might be a thief, but she's got nothing on you."

"I will pay you back, but not with Christmas. Now, it's time for us shake on it and move on." Father Christmas held his hand out to Krampus.

"Fool me once, shame on you..." Krampus growled and leaped through the air. He brought his birch sticks down across Father Christmas's outstretched hand.

"No!" Gabrielle leapt between Krampus and Father Christmas but Krampus shoved her off into the snow. Father Christmas roared with anger and his face turned as red as his robes as he bore down on Krampus.

"Stop!" Percival's voice cut through the wind. He thundered towards Krampus, his tiny hands balled into fists. Krampus cowered in mock terror, his birch sticks shaking as he bellowed with laughter. He straightened up and loomed over Percival. "And what exactly are you going to do, little-"

"Leave that boy alone!" Father Christmas's voice trembled with fury.

"There it is! Your pluck. Your courage. Your backbone. Congratulations, you've finally found them again." Krampus turned to Gabrielle. "But this charade is getting tired. Give me the key. Hand it over now, or I'll lock you away in a dungeon of eternal darkness and despair."

"Stay away from her!" Father Christmas threw his hand out and an unseen force struck Krampus and sent him sprawling into the snow.

# CHAPTER THIRTY-SEVEN

Stark dragged Gabrielle back as Krampus leaped to his feet. His claws clacked together as he clapped his hands slowly and his eyes blazed at Father Christmas. "A brawl then. A duel to decide this once and for all." He strode to his sleigh and removed a long black velvet sack. "We could try a test of strength but where would be the sport in that? And, it's Christmas Eve. What better night to exchange a gift or two?"

"Don't do this," Father Christmas said, his voice low. "I'm warning you."

"But I insist, old friend. I've gifts to give, and if you don't take them, I'll have to inflict them on your duplicitous friend." Krampus shot a dark look at Gabrielle as he reached into his sack. He pulled out a small box wrapped in charcoal colored paper and tied with a neat black bow. As he laid it upon the snow, he gestured for Father Christmas to take it. "Open it, I insist."

Father Christmas watched fearfully as the ribbon unfurled and the box sprung open to the din of broken kazoos. A tiny handheld mirror rose from the box and hovered before his long white beard.

"So you can see what you've become," Krampus purred. "Old, tired, lumpen and lardy, wheezy, flaky, blotched and tardy."

Shame dulled Father Christmas's eyes as he looked at his reflection. And then he shook his head. "Perhaps I should turn the mirror on you, Krampus? And treat you to a portrait of spite and envy."

"I'm sure I'd look as devilishly handsome as ever," Krampus countered. But his sneer was drawn and tired.

"Well now." Father Christmas reached into the sack at his feet. "Let's see what I've got in here for you." He presented a large box covered in candy-striped paper. "Here you are. I hope you enjoy them." Father Christmas snapped his fingers and the lid flew off.

Confetti and glitter showered the snow as something slithered from the box. It looked like a great brass snake, then Gabrielle heard it clank and rattle, and realized it was a long length of chain. It wriggled through the snow and wrapped itself around Krampus's feet, then rose around his legs. Krampus batted the chain away but it evaded his touch as it slithered up and coiled itself around his throat. One end bit the other, closing the circles it had formed around his neck and chest. "It burns!" Krampus howled. His face creased with agony. He tore at the chain. "Get it off me!"

"It will vanish..." Father Christmas said. "just as soon as you leave my lands."

"Keep him locked up!" Stark growled. "Evil..."

Krampus bent low and with a strange bellow his whole body heaved and shook. It took Gabrielle a moment to realize he was laughing. His eyes glowed like molten lava as he grasped the chain and snapped it in half. "I cannot be contained!" he roared. The broken links fell away, melted into the snow and vanished.

"Now then," Krampus said. "A sweet little something for you?" He reached into the black magical sack and smiled, but Gabrielle noticed the exhaustion in his eyes. The same exhaustion that dogged Father Christmas and she wondered if these mad conjurations were sapping their powers.

Father Christmas held up a hand, as if warding Krampus away.

"No," Krampus said. "I insist. You look so tired and hungry. Perhaps a little sugar will give your flagging powers a boost?" Krampus flickered like a ghost and for a moment Gabrielle could see the snow falling through his transparent form.

And then he was back with a wicked smirk as he produced a box wrapped in bile green paper. Krampus set it upon the ground and with a poof of black smoke a colossal plum pudding rose from the box. With a snap of his fingers the pudding burst alight with bright blue flames. It floated through the air and hovered before Father Christmas as if borne by ghostly hands. "No." He tried to push it away, but the pudding drew closer.

"You must have a taste, my friend!" Krampus clapped his hands and a silver spoon appeared. It dug itself into the pudding and sailed towards Father Christmas. He tried to bat it away but as he protested, it tipped the morsel into his mouth.

Father Christmas's anger turned to bewilderment, and then horror.

"I added a few fun surprises to the recipe." Krampus howled with laughter as the huge molded pudding broke apart and wriggling earthworms spilled out. They crackled in the flickering flames and burst upon the plate. "Indeed, it's no ordinary Christmas pudding," Krampus said. "But a feat of gastronomic science. Art, if you will. I call it *the death of Christmas.*"

Father Christmas clamped a hand over his mouth as a worm slipped through his fingers and wriggled into his beard. His face turned as scarlet as his tunic as he fixed Krampus with a vicious glare. "How dare you!" He flickered for a moment and vanished, then returned with a murderous glint in his eyes. He reached into his sack. "There must be something in here that will silence you for good!"

"They're going to destroy each other," Stark said.

Gabrielle stepped towards them. "Stop it. Please!"

Father Christmas shook his head, his smile edged with fury. "No. He's going to pay, even if it kills me." He wrenched a box wrapped in silver and green paper from the sack, tore it open and set it down at Krampus's feet. The lid flew up and the sides fell away, revealing a large glass snow globe. Inside there was a wintry hill with bright red flowers at its peak.

"Is that a...but you can't do..." Krampus began. "That's not fair!'"

And then he was gone.

"What happened? Where did he go?" Percival asked.

"There." Stark pointed to the globe. The glittery snow inside swirled around the hill and Gabrielle could see Krampus backing away from the lush poinsettia. He doubled over and retched, his eyes crimson as he staggered away from the flower. Krampus pounded a fist upon the glass and reached for his throat, his eyes watering as he stared out.

"I don't think he can breathe," Percival said as he picked up the globe and gave it a little shake.

"Don't fall for it," Father Christmas said. "There's plenty

of air in there. At least for now."

"I don't know...he looks pretty ill," Percival said as he held it up to his eye "Are you sure-"

"Yes, I am sure. And I will let him out...but if you had a dangerous spider in a jar you wouldn't just free it any old place. No, you'd find somewhere safe...and far away from your house." Father Christmas explained. "I'll take him back to his accursed mountain and his trolls will follow... then we will have Christmas back to..." Father Christmas doubled over and sneezed, and now Gabrielle could see the moonlight shining through his tunic.

"You're fading." She glanced to the snow globe. Krampus was sprawled upon his back, clasping his clawed hands to his translucent throat as he squirmed and gasped. "You're both..."

"They're killing each other!" Percival clutched the globe to his chest and ducked past Father Christmas.

"No." Father Christmas yelled. "Don't!"

But it was too late.

# CHAPTER THIRTY-EIGHT

Percival knocked the globe against the dark iron runner of the great black sled until it cracked. Krampus sprang to his feet and beat his fists against the glass as thick black smoke filled the globe. It billowed out through the narrow cracks and formed a giant horned silhouette in the air. Then the smoke faded and Krampus appeared in its wake. He winked at Percival, before glowering at Father Christmas. "So you'd kill me, would you?"

"No," Father Christmas shook his head. "I-"

"Tried to kill me. Don't deny it." Krampus flickered like television static and wagged his finger as he returned, looking wispy and nebulous. As if he wasn't really there. He staggered over to his sack and thrust a hand inside. "It's time for the final gift."

"No!" Gabrielle cried. "Stop it. Can't you see you're destroying yourselves?"

Krampus ignored her as he fished around, his tongue poking from the corner of his mouth, his face creased in rapt concentration. "You'll like this, old friend." He gave Father Christmas a bittersweet smile. "You wanted to retire. Well now you will have your wish."

*Wish...*

Gabrielle glanced up at Father Christmas as he stumbled away from Krampus. *He gave me a wish.* She'd planned to keep hold of it until she got back to the city. To use it to bring her parents together so she and Percival could leave that dark, cold place behind. But none of that mattered now. Because this was life or death.

Gabrielle closed her eyes, and put everything she had into her wish.

*Please work. You have to work.*

Fury etched Father Christmas's face as he delved into his sack, his form gossamer thin. "I have one final gift for you too, Krampus. One last thank you for your lies and treachery."

Krampus held out a wrapped box, but his snide grin faltered as the paper turned from a dung brown color to crisp white with merry scarlet polka dots. The bow flushed emerald green as it untied itself and the box sprang open to reveal a grand elegant cup. Spirals of fragrant steam wafted up from its golden rim, seasoning the air with the scent of rich hot drinking chocolate. Krampus clutched a hand over his nose, and retched. "I...didn't make this!"

Father Christmas gasped. Then his face turned from fearsome triumph to bewilderment as he held a box in his hands. Its paper turned as black as night and the silken ribbon unraveled to reveal a small ornate silver bucket filled with fiery red coals. "I didn't make this either."

Krampus cringed and held the cup out to Father Christmas as the sweet scent of the drinking chocolate prodded and overwhelmed his senses. "Take it, please!" he retched.

Father Christmas thrust the bucket of coals at him. "It's burning my fingers. Have them."

A ghost of a smile tugged Krampus's lips as he sniffed the pail. "It would be a shame to let such lovely coal go to waste. Unless I'm mistaken, these were lit in the fiery depths of Eldfell in Iceland. One of my favorite volcanos."

Father Christmas took a deep sip from his cup, leaving a line of chocolate upon his great mustache. "Exquisite! Where ever did you find it?" He took another gulp, and his features began to fill in until Gabrielle could no longer see the mountain through his robes.

"I've no idea," Krampus answered as he munched on another coal. "There are almost no words to describe how utterly delicious these are..." His ghostly fingers thickened as he reached inside the bucket for another morsel. He held it up and appraised it. "Seriously, they are perfect! How ever did you know?"

Father Christmas began to reply, but stopped and glanced at Gabrielle. She shook her head.

"That's my secret to keep. We're all entitled to one or two," Father Christmas winked.

"I take it this exchange was your doing?" Stark whispered to Gabrielle.

"I used my wish. They were destroying each other, and it was the only thing I could think of that might stop them."

"Very clever," Stark said. "I suppose one can not exist without the other. Just as there cannot be day without night."

Krampus burped and a puff of smoke escaped his lips. He clamped a hand over his mouth as Father Christmas gulped down the last of his chocolate. They stared at each other, then Krampus raised his coal bucket. Father Christmas did the same with his cup.

"A truce," Krampus said.

"A truce," Father Christmas agreed. They clinked the two vessels together, grinned and began to laugh, like old friends. Then a great din of bells echoed across the snowy waste and a frantic alarm rattled within the sack at Father Christmas's feet. "Oh dear!" he said, his smile fading. "It's happening!"

# CHAPTER THIRTY-NINE

"What is it?" Gabrielle asked as the bells chimed again and lights flashed across the sky in shades of ruby red and forest green.

"Christmas is coming" Stark said.

Father Christmas pulled an old fashioned alarm clock from the sack and squinted at it as if he couldn't quite believe what he was seeing. "We've got three hours." The corners of his lips turned down as he slipped the timepiece into the pocket of his robe.

"Let it go," Krampus said. "Start anew next year."

"I can't," Father Christmas said. "This is what I do, it's my purpose. People must have their wishes."

"There's not enough time," Krampus said. "What's done is done."

"I can't give up! I can't." Father Christmas turned to Stark. "How many presents have we got prepared?"

"Most of them," Stark said. "Save for one hundred and forty seven thousand. Give or take a gift or two. I mentioned this some time ago, but as I recall, you were preoccupied with a particularly large and messy trifle."

"One hundred and forty seven thousand gifts." Father Christmas gazed at the sky as it flashed again. "We could still do it. We'll have to run the machine at full steam, but we might just pull it off." He turned to Krampus. "Please tell me you didn't do anything to it while you were living in the palace."

"I assure you, I left it well alone," Krampus said. "It's a wretched, hideous thing. Grotesquely unstylish too."

"Then we still stand a chance of making and delivering the presents on time." Father Christmas's smile made him look younger, and more alive than Gabrielle had ever seen him. He rubbed his hands briskly. "Yes, we might still do it yet."

"I'll leave you to it." Krampus whistled for his wolves and climbed aboard his sleigh. "Good luck, old friend. I'll herd the trolls out of your kingdom, and round up the Christmas Cat too. Politely, of course."

"Don't forget Madam Grystle." A furrow troubled Father Christmas's brow. "You keep dark friends, Krampus."

"Indeed, and I wouldn't have it any other way." He raised a furry eyebrow at Gabrielle. "Hopefully she's recovered... after nearly drowning in her own soup." He cracked his reins and his wolves began to pad away.

"Stop!" Father Christmas shouted.

Krampus hissed to the wolves and they slowed. "What?"

"If fortune smiles on us, the Christmas machine will be able to finish the presents. But we'll never be able to deliver them all at this late hour. Not without help."

Krampus shook his finger. "I'm the dark side of Christmas,

remember, and you're the light. The stick and the carrot. And if this whole sorry episode has taught me one thing, its that we should keep to what we're best at."

"Hang on a minute." Percival said. "I saved you, I got you out of that snow globe."

"Yes, you certainly freed me from the overwhelming hideousness of that accursed poinsettia," Krampus agreed.

"Even though you made me scrub hundreds of grimy dishes, and unclog the drains. And comb the lice from that troll's beard,' Percival said. "I think you owe me."

Krampus gave Percival a wolfish grin. "When you put it like that, I suppose I do. So what do you want?"

"Help Father Christmas!"

*"That's all?"* Krampus nodded and shrugged. "Very well, I'll do it. Just this once." He nodded to Father Christmas. "I'll meet you at your infernal machine then. Hurry." He cracked the reins and the wolves took him soaring down the mountainside.

"Follow me." Father Christmas led Gabrielle, Percival and Stark to his sled. To a count of three they righted it and as they dusted away the snow that had gathered inside, Father Christmas raised his fingers to his lips and whistled. Moments later eight figures flew down through the snowy air. As the reindeer landed before him, they dipped their heads so he could fit their harnesses. Then Father Christmas climbed aboard the sled and motioned for Gabrielle, Percival and Stark to join him. "Quick. Time is of the essence."

Gabrielle and Percival sat upon the furs and grasped the rails of the sled. "Dash away!" Father Christmas called. The reindeer cantered down the hill. As they picked up speed they leaped into the air, taking the sled away with them.

They raced up through the falling snow and soared through the sky. Gabrielle peered over the side of the sled as the city of Christmas magically returned below them. The palace was a blur of color and movement, its walls turning from coal black to wintery white, its spikes becoming spires and the dark ominous horns shrank and faded away before her eyes.

The sled listed and shook as the reindeer circled around the glorious towers and dipped down over the courtyards. They slowed and alighted before the Christmas machine as it rumbled and shook in a cacophony of light and sound.

# CHAPTER FORTY

The Christmas machine was far larger and longer than Gabrielle had realized. She stared in amazement at its great silver conveyor belt stretching out into the darkness. Bleary eyed elves gathered around it, turning on lights and flicking switches. The machine whirred to life and she held her hands over her ears as its grind and clatter filled the night.

Father Christmas stood near the switchboard, holding up book after book as he called out names to Stark. The elf's fingers flew as he typed them out on a battered old typewriter. A tangle of copper tubes and wires connected it to the control panel of the machine, and the red and green lights blinked each time Stark pressed the return key.

Gabrielle had watched in wonder as Father Christmas loaded the expectant wishes into the machine earlier and she gasped as she'd caught sight of a few in their natural state.

They looked like tiny, glowing fairy lights, their brilliance compelling her to shield her eyes. It felt strange, she thought, to know she'd carried such a brilliant and lively thing in her heart each Christmas, without even knowing it was there.

The din rose as Father Christmas and Stark frantically added more and more names and instructions to the machine. Gabrielle peered through a metallic shutter in the side of the mechanism and caught a glimpse of all manner of curious, wonderful sights. Spinning clockwork and cogs, metallic hands with silver fingers that scrambled to arrange blocks of wood. Blades and guillotines that chopped with such speed that she could barely keep up with their movements. And round, robotic faces with glowing white eyes that meticulously oversaw the whole process.

Elves gathered along the conveyer belt to wrap the magical, bespoke trinkets, toys and baubles that emerged. Bright scraps of colored paper and ribbons littered the floor as they worked and a steady string of beautiful presents made their way along the line.

The trolls scampered and lurked at the very end, plucking the packages off the conveyer belt and loading them into large woolen sacks. Some of the bags were Krampus black, others were ruby red or forest green, but each seemed much larger on the inside than the out, judging by the hundreds upon hundreds of gifts the trolls had stuffed inside.

Gabrielle jumped as Father Christmas snapped his book shut and handed it to a waiting gnome who carried it back to the palace. "How many are still processing?"

Stark tapped a small glowing screen on the side of the typewriter. "Seven hundred and three."

Father Christmas pulled the alarm clock from his pocket. "We're running out of time." He yanked a lever on the side of the machine and it shook, jolted and groaned as steam burst from the vents. The needles spun and thrashed in its gauges and one of the arrows flew free, striking the glass case with such force, it cracked. "Faster!" Father Christmas cried. "Faster!"

The gears rattled, juddered and whined. Acrid smoke rose in plumes as the last of the presents jittered and flew down the conveyer belt. And then with one final burst of steam the whole thing groaned and jerked to a grinding halt. Flames erupted from its inner workings and the elves sprang to action, gathering snow in their hats to douse the fire, but it was too late as the whole contraption became engulfed by the blaze.

"Well, that's the end of that," Father Christmas said.

"Yes," Krampus agreed as he stepped from the shadows. "And good riddance. Ugly fiendish contraption. Although it definitely had its uses tonight." He gave a wan smile and joined Father Christmas as he walked alongside the conveyer belt. "But we must move onwards!"

The very last of the packages was whisked off the belt by an elf. She inspected them briefly, before tossing them to a troll who stuffed them into a sack. The Christmas Cat padded over and laid down so the troll could fasten the sack to the harness strapped across its back. The Cat narrowed its eyes and twitched its ears as it took the sack to the fleet of waiting sleighs.

Madam Grystle sauntered past Gabrielle with gifts piled up in her arms. She gave her a cruel hungry look, until Krampus cleared his throat.

"That's the last of them," Father Christmas called out. "Now get to the sleighs!"

"Can I ride with you?" Percival asked.

Father Christmas shook his head. Percival's face fell, until Father Christmas added, "I'd rather you had your own sled.

We need as many drivers out there as possible."

"Will mine have reindeer?" Percival grinned.

"I can't spare them," Father Christmas replied. "You'll have to take a motorized sleigh. Gabrielle can show you how to operate it, as I believe she's already familiarized herself with them."

Gabrielle felt her cheeks blush as she led Percival to a nearby sled and began to explain the controls. Krampus settled into his great black sleigh. Four trolls climbed in with him, each carrying sacks full of presents.

"Got that?" Gabrielle asked Percival.

He nodded. "It's easier than most of the games I play."

Gabrielle felt a twinge of anxiety and concern as she climbed into her sled, and glanced over at Percival as he took the seat in his. She wanted to ask Father Christmas if he would allow her to go with her brother, but time was running out and he was clearly preoccupied as he gave the alarm clock in his hand a worried look. "Is everyone ready?" His voice boomed. "It's going to be close, and if we miss delivering even a single present, the night will fail. Everyone must receive a wish if it's going to be Christmas. Everyone!"

"How do we deliver the presents?" Percival asked.

"There are goggles on your dashboards, put them on. They'll show you the houses that need gifts. They'll be the glowing ones." Father Christmas put his own goggles on, and Stark followed suit. "The glow will fade as soon as they've had their presents. Now, where you find chimneys, use them. They're easily the quickest way of dispatching gifts."

"But how do we know which present goes to which house?" Gabrielle asked.

Father Christmas smiled. "Reach into the sack and the correct gift will jump into your hands. Repeat this step until the all the bags are empty"

"Do we just throw the presents down the chimneys?"

Percival asked. "What if they have fires burning in their fireplaces?"

Father Christmas pulled a present from his sack and held it up. "The wrapping paper is enchanted. It won't burn."

"Right," Percival said. Then his brow furrowed once more. "But how do we get the presents into the stockings, or under the Christmas trees?"

Father Christmas set a gift upon the snow. A pair of wrapping paper arms and legs burst from the sides, and it stood and scuttled across the snow. The gift reached up and climbed onto Father Christmas's sled and dived into the sack. "That's how." Father Christmas's smile faltered as he gazed back at the clock. "Percival and Gabrielle are going to the places they're familiar with. Krampus and his trolls will cover the South. The elves and I will cover the rest of the world." He clapped his hands and glanced into the sky. "To your sleighs. Buckle up and don't delay."

"Oh," Gabrielle said, as a great circle appeared in the sky, its edges swirling blue and mauve. The air in the center flickered like a heat haze and a town with slanted rooftops appeared, a giant clocktower loomed over them and stars twinkled in the night sky. "That one's mine." Krampus cracked his reins and the wolves leaped, carrying the sleigh up into the air and right through the vortex. It shimmered and gave a loud pop, like a cork pulled from a bottle. Now Gabrielle could see a seaside town with twinkling lights and stuccoed houses along the hillsides. Madam Grystle soared up and passed through the vortex, then the scene shifted to a familiar looking town with a wintry park bordered by wooden houses with picket fences.

"Is that-" Percival began.

"Your home," Father Christmas said. "And I'm sure you know every single shortcut."

"I do," Percival said, with no small pride.

"Then off you go!"

Percival pushed the 'Up' button and shoved the lever forward on his sled. It lurched up and shot through the vortex. The scene changed and Gabrielle saw her uncle's city, and the snow capped mountains that surrounded it.

"Fly, Gabrielle Greene!" Father Christmas called.

She pushed the 'Up' button and slid the lever. Her sleigh jolted through the air and soared into the heart of the vortex.

Lights rushed and danced around her as she passed from the land of Christmas, back to the world she'd left behind.

# CHAPTER FORTY-ONE

The city had changed since Gabrielle's return to Christmas. The dark clouds and endless rain were gone, replaced by thick layers of gleaming white snow. The streets were no longer lined with the ominous tatty black ribbons that had hung like stringy crow feathers. Now they were festooned with bright green and silver tinsel. And everywhere, flashing lights.

Gabrielle glanced at the clock mounted to the front of the sled as she pulled on the goggles that had rested on the seat beside her.

*Four minutes past eleven.*

A long row of numbers ticked below the clock, counting down as presents were delivered around the world. The numbers moved lightning fast, but there were still so many gifts left to deliver and time was running out.

Gabrielle pulled the lever and sent the sled speeding down to the closest house. The roof and chimney glowed with bright golden light, so Gabrielle dropped a present from the sack. As it sailed down the chimney, another jumped into her hand. She dropped this one too and then another, until finally the glowing light dimmed and vanished.

She sped to the next house and filled its chimney with gifts, before soaring across the street. This house had no chimney, so she dipped down and tossed a present toward the porch. It hit the snow and lay still, before tiny paper arms and legs popped from the box and took it skittering to the front door. The present scaled up the door, opened the letterbox and posted itself. Gabrielle dropped five more gifts there, before the house's glowing walls dimmed and winked out.

The next house had no chimney and no letterbox. As she threw the gifts, they flattened themselves, zipped through the air like frisbees, and slipped under the door. Gabrielle raced back up into the air and made her way to the next street.

A well dressed couple emerged from a taxi below. They glanced up and Gabrielle waved. The man waved back, but the woman pulled his arm down. They exchanged words, then they looked back up and their faces were perfectly blank. As if nothing strange or out of the ordinary had just happened.

The clock ticked on, and while the line of numbers kept spiraling down, there was still so much to do.

Gabrielle's heart thumped hard as a great popping sound issued from the flickering vortex and Percival's sleigh appeared. He raced down and drew alongside her. "I finished delivering the presents and then the portal brought me here. Do you need help?"

"Yes! There's still too many presents!" Gabrielle called back as she raced to the next house; a small shack on the edge of the city. She threw a gift from the sack and it flew down, its wrapping paper arms and legs held out like a parachutist in free fall. The gift rolled over in the snow, leaped to its feet, and dived through the mail slot.

"Give me some!" Percival called. Gabrielle reached back and pulled a sack free and passed it over to him. Percival hauled it into his sled raced toward the other side of town.

Gabrielle sped along, making her deliveries as fast as she could but the clock steadily ticked the time away.

She gazed from the distant line of glowing roofs to the clock, her heart thumping hard. There were so many houses left, and simply not enough time. *Three minutes to midnight.*

It was impossible.

Gabrielle watched as Percival zipped through the air, his tongue protruding from the side of his mouth, his face rapt with concentration. He dropped the last of his presents and zipped back to join her.

"There's still too many! I'm not going to make it." Gabrielle swept into the street and shot between two parked cars. She dug into the sack and pulled out a present wrapped in purple paper. It landed on the lawn before her with a thump and jumped up and sprinted to the house, as if it too knew the clock was ticking.

Gabrielle flew up and dug another gift from the sack. She hurtled it over the side and sped away before it had even neared the chimney.

The minute hand inched towards midnight.

"I can't do it!" Gabrielle shouted. "I wish we'd..." She froze, and a chill passed across her shoulders. "The wish! Percival, you've probably still got one. Use it!"

"How?"

"Make a wish that I'll deliver the presents before midnight. Quick!"

A strange, pensive look crossed Percival's face. "I've got a wish…"

Gabrielle could see the conflict upon his face. No doubt he was dreaming of endless boxes of colored pens, firecrackers and ships in bottles. "Please, Percival. Hurry!"

The hand ticked closer, it was almost upon the hour.

"I wish…" Percival glanced from Gabrielle to his feet. He shook his head and closed his eyes. "I wish Gabrielle had more time."

Suddenly everything stopped. Percival's sled hung over the rooftops, his hair floated in a halo around his head and the snowflakes were fixed in midair. It looked as if he was an actor in a movie that had been paused.

Gabrielle hurtled on through the icy sky.

The clock hand froze in that final notch, just before midnight and only the numbers continued to count down.

*Seven. Six. Five…*

A single snowflake moved past Gabrielle's head, white and fragile and crystalline.

"Hurry!" Gabrielle cried as she bolted over the last few houses, hurling handfuls of presents toward the chimneys.

*Four. Three…*

The sled shook as Gabrielle pushed the lever as far as it would go.

She raced towards the final house and stuffed her hand into the sack. Her fingers shook as she wrenched out the final gift and threw it.

It hit the chimney and fell upon the roof.

*Two…*

The gift leaped up, but there wasn't time.

Gabrielle jumped over the side of the sled and landed

hard upon the roof. Her feet slid out from under her as she grabbed the gift by its papery arm and flung it over the side of the chimney.

The glow around her flickered, and faded and Gabrielle gasped as she slid over the edge of the roof.

Before she could even scream, she was tumbling down toward the icy concrete patio.

Gabrielle closed her eyes as she landed hard on a pile of furs. She looked over to find Percival sitting before her steering his sled. He took it soaring down and landed in the snowy yard. "You did it!" he cried as he pointed to the clock.

"We did it," Gabrielle cried out.

"Yes we did!" Krampus said as he swooped down alongside and gave her a wide, wolfish smile.

"By the skin of your teeth!" Father Christmas's boomed as he joined them. "Gabrielle Greene, the girl who saved Christmas."

"And stole it twice," Krampus said, his eyes gleaming mischievously. "Now, this mutual back slapping is as touching as it is nauseating. But that being said, I can't pretend I'm not a little relieved to have things back the way they should be."

"Thank you," Father Christmas said. "I think."

Krampus shrugged and his forked tongue shot out and caught a flea as it leaped down his arm. He popped it into his mouth and bit down hard. "Say no more. Literally."

"So what happens now?" Percival asked. "And what about next year's presents? Are you going to need help making them, now your machine's broken?" He tried, and failed, to keep his voice nonchalant.

"I think we can manage" Father Christmas clapped his hand upon Percival's shoulder. "But I'll keep your offer in mind if the time comes. Besides, you've done more than enough. Both you and your sister. Now climb into my sleigh and I'll take you back to your uncle's house where you can have a long, well deserved rest and dream bright dreams and wake to a beautiful Christmas Day. And I've a feeling it's going to be a good one this year."

"May I join you?" Krampus said. "I have a spot of unfinished business in that neighborhood."

"Really?" Father Christmas raised a bushy eyebrow.

*"Pleasant* unfinished business," Krampus said. "For the most part."

Gabrielle and Percival climbed into Father Christmas's sled and the reindeer took them soaring up over the rooftops.

# CHAPTER
# FORTY-TWO

Gabrielle's stomach fluttered as they swept down to land upon the snowy lawn in front of their uncle's house. She stepped unsteadily from the sled, and was barely through the door when Matilda appeared.

"Where have you been?" Matilda demanded, her arms folded tightly over her green pajamas and her silvery braces flashing as she scowled.

"We..." Gabrielle glanced back at Krampus and Father Christmas. "Can you see them?"

"See who?" Matilda asked. "Don't try and pull that baloney on me again. I asked you where you've been-" Her face fell.

*'Now* she sees us.' Krampus waved his hand through the air. "And we see her."

"Who are..." Matilda's mouth fell open.

"He's the nice one." Krampus nodded to Father Christmas. "And I'm the nasty one." He stepped past Gabrielle and ran his hands through Matilda's hair, causing it to stand on end. Then he leaned down and peered into her eyes with a vicious smile. "If I were one to observe the rules, I wouldn't dare mention the yearly visits you used to make to my lands and the mines below Krampus mountain. As it happens, when it comes to rules, I'm always willing to make exceptions." He tapped a gnarly finger against Matilda's forehead. "If I hear you've even thought about harassing your dear cousins, I'll pay you a visit. In the dead of night. With a bag full of nightmares to remind you of what you'd forgotten." He clapped his hands, "But...ah...I see it's coming back. Now you remember."

"You..." Dim recognition passed across Matilda's face. She turned and bolted through the house.

"There we go." Krampus turned to Percival and shook his hand, before bowing to Gabrielle. "I'll take my leave and wish you farewell, I have one final visit before I return to the shadows and gloom. Be good Gabrielle and Percival Greene. Or...don't...if you'd like to see me again." He smiled as he flitted through the front door and vanished into the night.

. . .

Uncle Florian sat slumped in his living room chair, his wheezing snores punctuated by his panicked breaths. Gabrielle felt her shoulders fall. He looked shattered. On the table before him sat a number of tiny boxes, wrapped in paper that looked like it had been saved from an old long forgotten Christmas.

"There rests a broken man," Father Christmas said with a bittersweet smile. "And I know what that's like."

"He lost his business," Percival said.

"Such a shame," Father Christmas replied. "I've known

dear Florian for many, many years. He's a good man who has always used his wishes for everyone but himself."

"Can you help him?" Gabrielle asked.

"If only I could. But I cannot compel people to buy his clocks or things they don't wish to buy. That would be wrong."

"There must be something you can do," Gabrielle said.

"I'm afraid not." Father Christmas shook his head. "Except hold on to the hope that he'll spend his next wish on good things for himself, for a change."

"We can tell him to use his wish!" Percival said.

Father Christmas shook his head. "Oh no, I'm afraid you'll forget everything by morning. That's how it works."

"But...we just wish things were better for him." Gabrielle said.

"I have a very strong feeling they will be. Now, speaking of wishes..." Father Christmas leaned down and shook their hands one by one. Then he dug into his pocket and gave each of them a small gift wrapped in red and white polka dotted paper. He gasped as he glanced at the old grandfather clock. "It's late now and I must be getting back. Open your gifts and if you are ready, make your wishes tonight, lest you forget. Then it's off to bed. Sleep well, and enjoy a most wonderful Christmas Day. Savor it, for who knows how much longer you'll be in this fair city." He winked, hugged them and strode to the front door as he called out "Merry Christmas Gabrielle and Percival Greene!"

And then he was gone.

. . .

Percival unwrapped his gift, his tongue protruding from the side of his mouth and his brow furrowed. Beneath the wrapping paper was a small wooden lion. It opened its chocolate-brown mouth and gave a tiny roar, before winking and becoming a statue once more.

"Make your wish," Gabrielle said, but she saw that Percival's eyes were already screwed shut. He opened them and gave a sleepy grin, followed by a long, loud yawn.

"Open yours," Percival said.

Gabrielle carefully peeled the paper away. She wanted to save it, hoping somehow that it might help her remember everything. If that was possible. Nestled within the folds of the wrapping paper she found a wooden key, just like the one she'd stolen and given to Krampus. The warm polished finish flashed gold for a moment, before transforming back to wood. "The key to Christmas." Gabrielle smiled and closed her eyes, and made her wish.

. . .

By the time she woke the next morning, Gabrielle had forgotten everything. She climbed out of bed and found herself grinning, even though she had absolutely no idea why. The only thing she knew, was that she'd had the strangest, most vivid dreams. Of sleds and snowy forests, of all manner of bizarre creatures gathered around a tree covered in gleaming stars. And each star had been a wish-

Someone knocked upon the door. It opened and Uncle Florian's hand appeared, clutching a phone. "It's for you."

Gabrielle placed the phone against her ear.

"Gabs?"

Happiness flooded through Gabrielle as she heard her mother's voice, swiftly followed by a flash of anger.

"Merry Christmas."

"Merry Christmas," Gabrielle responded dully, summoning as much enthusiasm as she could. "Where are you?"

"In a hotel."

"Oh. She said as her heart sank. "Where's Dad?"

"He's right here."

"Oh. Are you on holiday? I hope you're having a nice time." Gabrielle shivered. The room was freezing.

"Yes. We've sorted everything out, love. And Uncle Florian's coming to pick us up. We flew in late last night and got a room by the airport."

"Really?" Gabrielle's anger began to melt away along with the sadness she hadn't realized she'd carried for so long.

"Really! Now your dad wants to speak to you, then pass us over to Percy. See you soon, and Merry Christmas!"

Gabrielle grinned as she gazed through the window and waited for her father to pick up the phone. Everything outside shone soft and white, and in that moment, Gabrielle Greene felt as if everything would finally be okay.

. . .

No one, apart from Percival, heard the knock upon the front door. His head popped up as his parents, Uncle Florian and Gabrielle continued to play cards and Matilda gazed at the television like a zombie. Although she'd actually been nice today. She'd even smiled at him as she'd shared her chocolates. Which was beyond strange even if it was Christmas Day.

The knock came again.

Percival wandered to the front door and opened it to a blast of cold air. A box wrapped in licorice black paper, sat outside the empty doorway. The card stuck to the top depicted a dark mountain with a pair of colossal stone horns upon its peak. Something about the image filled Percival with a surge of dread, but he shook his head to dispel it.

He felt confident today, filled with the certainty that he'd accomplished something mighty and bold. But he couldn't quite remember what it was, so he chalked it up to the curious dream that had filled his sleep. The one with the ruddy faced elves and trolls, giant cats and lots and lots of snow.

And a tree, a tree filled with stars...

Percival stooped down and picked up the box. He flipped the card open to find a message in neat, curved handwriting:

"To Percival, the boy who saved me from the stench of Christmas.

Your friend, K"

"K?" Percival slipped his finger under the wrapping paper and opened it slowly.

The box was filled with candies wrapped in twisted black and white striped paper and resting among them was a glass bottle with an intricate wooden ship inside.

"*The* ship in a bottle." Percival's fingers trembled as he held it up to see the tiny captain standing at his wheel and the sailors tending the riggings as they awaited orders that would take them off to magical lands.

"Thank you!" Percival whispered, even though he wasn't exactly sure who he was whispering to. But as he glanced into the street, he spotted a trail of peculiar hoof prints among the crisp black coal dust that glittered atop the gleaming white snow.

## THE END

If you enjoyed this book there's also a short story related to the world in this novel called *The Night of the Christmas Letter-Getters* which you can find in most online book shops.

# Additional books by Eldritch Black

The Book of Kindly Deaths

## Short Stories

The Night of the Christmas Letter-Getters
One Dark Hallow's Eve
The Curious Incident at Gloamingspark Yard
The Ghosts of The Tattered Crow
Three Curses for Trixie Moon
The Festival of Bad Tidings

# Author Note

Thank you so much for reading Krampus & The Thief of Christmas. I hope you enjoyed the story as much as I enjoyed making it up. Or did I? I'll leave that for you to discover...

I'd be over the moon (and Jupiter) if you could leave me a quick review of this book on Amazon! It doesn't have to be long or complicated, but if you could write a sentence or two about what you enjoyed, that would be wonderful. Reader reviews are incredibly important to us scribblers!

All the best!
Eldritch Black

## About the Author

Eldritch Black is an author of darkly whimsical tales of gothic dread and fantastical horror. His first novel 'The Book of Kindly Deaths' was published in 2014, and he's also produced a number of short stories.

Eldrich was born in London, England and now lives in the woods on a small island near Seattle. When he isn't writing, Eldritch enjoys collecting ghosts, forgotten secrets and lost dreams.

*Connect with Eldritch:*

Twitter
@EldritchBlack

Facebook:
www.facebook.com/EldritchBlackAuthor/

www.eldritchblack.com

Made in the USA
Middletown, DE
02 December 2016